Hickory Dickory Dock The Ghost In The Clock

Janet McNulty

Hickory Dickory Dock The Ghost In The Clock

Copyright © 2016 Janet McNulty
Cover Illustration by Robert Henry

ISBN-10: 1-941488-71-4
ISBN-13: 978-1-941488-71-3

For all those who love grandfather cloccks.

Hickory Dickory Dock
The Ghost In The Clock

Chapter 1

I stepped out the doors of the Fine Arts Center of the campus, enjoying the fresh, warm air that greeted me as I walked down the concrete walkway, looking forward to dumping my book bag in my car and starting my summer vacation. Though I would be working at the Candle Shoppe all summer, I managed to get out of having to take any summer courses. What a relief. For a while there, during the semester, I thought I was going to have to retake one of my classes, but managed to squeak out of there with a passing grade. Some of my later courses have been difficult—and I thought my first year of college was hard.

A horn honked as I reached the parking lot and Jackie's voice carried across the asphalt as she called to me from the passenger window of Greg's car. I waved back at her and she crawled into the back seat as I got in.

"So," she said, "how was your last day?"

"Exhausting," I replied.

"Really?"

"No," I laughed at her. "Just a relief to have it all done. Now I can relax all summer."

"That's what you think," said Jackie. "I heard that Mr. Stilton is thinking of taking some time off and leaving us in charge of the store."

Was she serious? I had never known Mr. Stilton to take any time off and for him to go on a vacation was news, and a bit unnerving. I have never run a store before, aside from closing up or opening, and neither had Jackie, and I would never leave Tammy in charge.

"Enough about school and work," said Greg as he pulled out of the parking lot, doing his best to avoid other college students who ambled in the crosswalk, spending more time staring at their phones than paying attention to where they were going. "Here."

He handed me three tickets and I gave one to Jackie. For the past year, the city had been building a Municipal Amusement Center, a place where children and adults could go to have fun, geared mostly towards families with children, but they had a few things that adults would like. It had opened last month, but with finals, Greg and I hadn't had a chance to go. Now that the semester had ended, we were free to check it out. He must have picked up the tickets right after I had left for my last final.

Jackie took hers and did an enthusiastic dance in the back seat.

"I've never known you to like amusement parks so much," I teased her.

She smacked me with her ticket.

"Hey, you two," joked Greg, "I'll turn this car around."

Jackie settled back into her seat with a huff while I tried to contain my laughter.

Greg pulled onto the freeway and drove ten miles to the exit that took us to the amusement park. It appeared that we were not the only ones with the idea of going as the line of cars on the off-ramp went all the way to the interstate. Greg took his place in a line that moved at a steady pace; which was good because more cars lined up behind us.

"I don't see any of those rides that make you sick," said Jackie.

Probably a good thing, but I didn't tell Jackie that. She loved the rides that spun you around in 20 different directions and made you so dizzy and sick that you can barely stand, at least, that's what they did to me. I looked up and saw the Zipper Ride and pointed it out to Jackie. "There you go."

Jackie beamed.

Greg found a parking space and we all got out of the car and walked to the gate where we handed the kid stationed there our tickets. The teenager—and I could tell by his bored demeanor that this was just a summer job to him—scanned our tickets, which looked like credit cards, and gave them back to us.

"Enjoy the park," he said in a flat tone.

"Wow," commented Jackie, "he doesn't sound too thrilled to be here."

"You wouldn't be either if this was your job," I reminded her.

"Good point."

We moseyed down the green walkway to the central plaza of the park, taking a look at the rides, the food stands—Jackie's eyes lit up at the funnel cake one while Greg seemed more interested in the fried hot dog stand—and the various games that were offered with their larger than life prizes. Parents with their children, most of whom looked like they had just gotten out of school themselves, wandered around, seeing what was there before deciding on what they wanted to do first. Some of the younger ones tugged on their parents' arms, pulling them in several directions, wanting on go on every ride and play every game all at once.

The sounds of thrilled screams met our ears as we strayed past the Tilt-a-Whirl and continued following the main walkway. Just watching the separate cars twirl around in rapid circles make me want to retch.

"Hey, look!" Jackie ran ahead of us a little.

In the center of the park's plaza stood a grandfather clock, and it looked custom made as it was larger than the average one, surrounded by tables and chairs filled with people lounging or taking the time to eat something.

"That is unusual," said Greg as he walked up to the placard in front of the clock. "Archibald Wilson's clock. Donated by the Wilson family."

"That says a lot," muttered Jackie. "I think it might be broken."

"It looks like a genuine clock and not a modern reproduction," said Greg as he studied it further.

"That is because it is genuine," said a deep voice.

We all jumped a bit and turned to find a man in a custodial uniform standing behind us.

"Didn't mean to startle you," he said.

"Not at all"—I glanced at his nametag—"Jeb."

He smiled at my boldness.

"You work here?" asked Greg.

"Yes," replied Jeb. "I'm just a janitor here. Help keep the place clean, but I noticed you all looking at this clock and thought I would tell you to not touch it."

Greg pulled his hand off the side of the clock and stepped away when Jeb pointed out the *Please Do Not Touch* sign. "Sorry," he mumbled.

"Oh, you're not the first one to ignore that sign. These things don't exist much today with everything being digital and all."

"So this is a real grandfather clock?" asked Greg.

"Yes," replied Jeb. "This one was made in 1835. You can tell by the design there on the clock face. Grandfather clocks were first invented around 1670 and built up until the 20th century, and until the invention of the digital clock, they were the premier and most reliable way to tell time. This particular clock belonged to an Archibald Wilson. He lived from 1887-1976. His family inherited his estate and this clock sat in a storage facility up until last year when the family decided to sell and or donate what was there. Lucky for this park, they decided to donate it here."

"But it doesn't work," said Jackie.

"We have a guy coming in to fix that. He's a clocksmith and will be here after the park closes at ten."

"That's a bit late," Greg commented.

"It's what he wanted. He says it's easier to work on clocks when people aren't gawking at it."

I scanned the area and observed two children playing tag around the clock.

"Now, now," said Jeb in a calm, but firm manner, "don't play around or touch this clock, please. There's a playground over there if you wish to chase each other."

Disappointed looks crossed the two kids' faces, but they ran off to the playground that had been set aside with jungle gyms, monkey bars, swings, and a few other things kids like to play on.

"Well, I need to get back to work," said Jeb, waving good-bye. "You all have fun now."

"So, what do you guys want to do?" asked Jackie before changing her mind. "You know what? Never mind. Why don't we go our separate ways for now and meet back here in a couple of hours?"

"Sounds good to me," said Greg.

"Perfect," Jackie replied. "And, uh, stay out of trouble." Jackie gave me a knowing look and I stared at her, since in the last few years it seemed that I either found trouble, or trouble found me.

"Scout's honor," I told her, raising my right hand and using my left to cross my heart.

Jackie gave me a disbelieving look. "Two hours, peeps!"

Greg and I watched her leave and I hoped she wouldn't be bored being by herself, but she had insisted that she would be fine with giving Greg and I a chance to be alone for a while, and she liked to go on those rides that flip you around which I couldn't do anymore, not without getting nauseated. So we all had agreed on two hours, when we would meet back up and get something to eat.

"So, what do you want to do?" asked Greg?

"The Ferris Wheel?"

He tilted his head.

"You want something with a bit more excitement?"

Greg nodded.

"Maybe I should have sent you with Jackie."

He laughed and gave me a kiss. "It's okay."

"How about the Flyers, then."

Greg smiled, holding his hand out for me and we wandered over to the Flyers, getting in the long line. The ride was more popular than I thought it would be, but at least it moved along at a quick pace and we were able to get a seat after two runs. With all day passes, we didn't have to purchase a fistful of red tickets to get on the ride. We just had to swipe the passes on the scanner. I took the seat behind Greg, since they were one-seaters, and my stomach lurched a bit when I felt my feet leave the ground as we were suspended in the air. Being on the ride brought back memories of when Jackie and I were in grade school and our parents took us to the Summer Fair each year, until were reached high school and decided we could go ourselves. I remembered we always loved this ride and the drop tower ones.

I glanced at Greg and noticed him reach up. Oh, no! He was going to do it. Just as the cable slacked a little, which it does sometimes, he snapped it, causing a jolt to run through all of the cables to everyone's seat. Another person snapped his. Before I knew it, almost everyone snapped their cables, much to the ire of the attendant who got a sour look on his face. Okay, then, two can play at this game. I waited for just the right moment when the cable to my seat would slacken and I snapped it, giving it a good bounce. I heard Greg's laughter from up ahead. I don't think he expected me to do that. The ride slowed and my seat lowered as it ended, allowing my feet touched the ground once again.

"I didn't think you had it in you to do that," Greg teased me when I met him at the ride's exit gate.

"You started it and I finished it. Come on, they have bumper cars over there."

I led him over to what I had called bumper cars, but in reality, it was bumper boats, but I didn't care. A giant pool had been made with tiny, single seater boats put in it and the people on that ride looked to be having a lot of fun. Once again, we took our place in line and worked our way to the front, swiping our passes, and getting our boats. Greg pretended to rev his engine, making *VROOM! VROOM!* sounds, which made me and some of the kids laugh. A few of the parents around us chuckled as well. The light turned green and a buzzer sounded, meaning that it was time to play.

I rammed my boat into Greg, pushing him against the side of the pool. His surprised expression told me that he had not expected that, but I knew I would regret it. After a few seconds, when I had worked my way to the other side, after ramming into a few other people, Greg plowed into me from behind and somehow managed to splash the water, getting me wet. In retaliation, as he rode past with a smirk, I reached over the side of my boat and splashed water on him.

"Keep your hands inside the boats!" yelled the attendant.

Oops. It appeared that I had started something, because at that moment people stopped bumping into one another and began splashing water on each other, turning the bumper boats ride into a gigantic water fight. Even some of the parents got in on the action. The less-than-amused attendant sounded the buzzer and flashed the red light, signaling that the ride had ended and everyone was forced to return their boats and disembark. He glowered at Greg and me as we walked past and I snorted in an effort to contain my laughter.

"Hey you two!"

We turned around just as Elise ran up to us with Tiny right behind her holding a gigantic, stuffed pink bunny rabbit. He made quite a sight walking around dressed in black leather and carrying that oversized stuffed animal in his brawny arms, with the tattoos stretching down them.

"Hi, Elise," I said.

"Looks like you caught something there," Greg said in a joking manner, receiving a glare from Tiny in response.

"He won it for me at the game over there," Elise said, pointing at a booth. "Oh, quit acting like that," she told Tiny, giving him a playful smack. "Carrying that thing around won't ruin your reputation as a hardened tough guy."

Tiny grunted in response.

"No more than those tights from a few months ago when the circus was in town," laughed Greg and I shushed him when Tiny's face turned plum purple in response. I will never be able to apologize enough for that mistake.

"You two should join us," said Elise. "We're going to the Tunnel of Love next."

"I don't really want to bring this thing with us," Tiny said, holding up the stuffed bunny.

"Oh, it won't be so bad," chided Elise. "Besides…" She leaned over and whispered something in Tiny's ear which made his eyes light up.

"Whatever you say, babe," Tiny whispered back to her.

"We're supposed to meet up with Jackie soon," I said, "but you two have fun. We'll see you around."

Tiny and Elise waved and hurried off to the Tunnel of Love and Greg winked at me, gesturing in that direction, just as a small train filled with kids and adults tooted past us.

"We should go on that," I suggested, "and maybe the mini-rollercoaster afterward." I pointed at the area where the tiny rollercoaster ride was that had a few up as and downs, but did not go very high off the ground since little kids were allowed on it.

"Oh, I suppose," Greg conceded.

For the next hour, we tried out a few rides, played a couple of carnival games (which Greg had managed to win me a lamp-sized, green, stuffed bird) before heading over to the grandfather clock to meet up with Jackie and who should I see with her, but—Tammy. Jackie stood there with her arms folded, looking nonplussed, and relief flooded her face when Greg and I showed up.

"Mel!" screeched Tammy, running towards me, but I stepped out of the way of her charge, forcing her to run past a few steps where she collided with a park employee.

"Where did you…" I started to ask Jackie, but she interrupted me.

"Don't even get me started."

"Jackie saved me," Tammy said to me, her face flushed from her short sprint.

"Saved you?" I replied.

"Yep! I wanted to go on the Zipper, but you have to have a partner with you and no one wanted to ride with me."

"I wonder why," Jackie whispered in my ear.

"But I saw Jackie here," Tammy continued, "and she offered—"

"Not how I remember it," Jackie muttered.

"—to be my partner on the ride so that I could go. We had so much fun!"

A snort escaped Jackie's mouth while Greg tried to hold back a fit of laughter, but his red face and bulging cheeks exposed his thoughts.

"It's nice to see you, Tammy," I said, "but we need to get going."

"Oh, let me come with you!" Tammy seized my arm and yanked me towards her.

"Uh…" I began, but at that moment she noticed someone that she must have known because she released my arm, causing me to fall backward, and ran off.

"Hey, Lia, wait up!"

"You okay?" Greg asked me.

"I'll be fine." I turned to Jackie. "How did you run into her, again?"

Jackie released an exasperated sigh and folded her arms. "I was standing in line at the Zipper with a guy who had agreed to be my partner on it when she came out of nowhere and pulled me out of the line, dragging me to the front, and before I knew it, we both were locked in this cage and spinning through the air!"

"Well, at least you got to go on one of your favorite rides."

"I didn't want to go on it with her!"

"So, what happened to the guy you were with?"

"What do you think? Tammy scared him away and I didn't see him after we got off the ride."

I patted Jackie on the back, feeling bad for her. I knew how Tammy's overexcited nature tended to scare people away.

"Why don't we just enjoy the rest of our day," I suggested.

That is just what we did. We went on a few more rides, including the train, visited the fried hot dog and funnel cake stands, before going to some of the performances they had. Only when the sun started to dip behind the horizon did we decide to go home.

Exhaustion swept over me after we left the park, not the kind where you feel worn out, but the kind where you know you had a great time with the people you care about, and best of all, there were no ghosts.

Chapter 2

I woke up the next morning with my phone ringing; it's incessant screams jolting me from my bed as I fell out and scrambled around in a desperate attempt to shut it up. "Hello?" I said, my voice heavy and hoarse from sleep.

"Miss Summers?"

I recognized that voice and the person behind it: Detective Shorts. "Yes?" My eyes popped open as I became more awake.

"I need your assistance. Are you able to meet me down at the amusement park in the next 20 minutes?"

I glanced at my bare feet and the mangled pajamas that covered my body, not wanting to even think about what my hair looked like. "Can we make it 35?"

"I'll see you in 20. Meet me at the entrance gate." He hung up.

Okay, 20 it is then.

I shot out of bed and ran to the bathroom, throwing my hair into a ponytail, my old standby hairstyle, splashed some cool water on my face to wake up, before running back to my bedroom where I grabbed the clothes I had worn the day before out of my laundry basket and threw them on. I sniffed a sleeve and reeled back, but didn't have time to find something more suitable. I hope he doesn't mind the ripe smell. I glanced at the clock in my room, amazed that only five minutes had ticked by in my mad dash to get dressed. I guess it is possible to get ready in such a short amount of time, if you don't mind look-ing like a train wreck and smelling like a rotted banana dipped in grease.

Shoving my phone in my back shorts pocket, I snatched my wallet and keys and hurried out the door. I rushed down the hallway and the stairs to the parking area, pressing the unlock button on my key and listening for the familiar chirp as my car responded. Before the sun had a chance to greet the world, I was on the road and headed for the interstate.

Detective Shorts waited for me by the entrance gates just like he said he would, dressed in his usual attire of a cheap, department store suit. How did he manage to always wear a jacket, even when it was warm, and never break a sweat? I shook the question from my mind when I saw his unhappy, or maybe he was just tired, expression. The other police cars with their flashing lights and uni-formed officers walking around, not to mention a cou-ple people from the medical examiner's office carrying a gurney, told me that this was not a social call, not that I needed police cars to inform me of that. Detective Shorts never made social visits. He was all business.

I parked to the side of the entrance, not bothering to pull into an actual parking space. Detective Shorts was by the driver's side of my door before I managed to turn off the engine.

"Morning," I greeted him as I stepped out of the car.

"Miss Summers, follow me please."

That's it? Not even a hello?

"What is this all about?" I asked him.

"You will see," replied Detective Shorts as he walked towards the entrance gate and I followed him through it, wondering why he had called me so early in the morning. He never asked for my assistance in an investigation before and spent most of his time telling me to stay out of it. I guess, this time, he hoped to head me off, knowing I would probably find out about this incident sooner than later.

We walked through the park and towards the central plaza where the grandfather clock was, it's ornate shape casting long shadows in the early morning sunlight, as the sun had now risen. I watched as police officers marked off the area around the clock with yellow tape that had the word "caution" on it, while others took pictures of the scene, wondering why they were all gathered around the clock itself. As I followed the detective, I remembered that Jackie, Greg, and I had been there yesterday and were remarking at the antiquity of the clock and how it stood apart from the rest of the park and its modern flair.

Detective Shorts ducked, walking underneath the tape and held it up for me to pass beneath it. I did.

"Why am I…"

I stopped speaking when Detective Shorts waved his hand at the clock and inside I saw the body of a man, but more a midget, or dwarf, instead of a full-sized man. Graying facial hair covered his face and his hands and legs looked strange, which is normal when you see little people, their stunted growth always looking odd when compared to normal-sized individuals. He was tucked away quite nicely in the belly of the clock, except that he was also dead.

I looked at Detective Shorts. Shouldn't he be telling me to stay out of this?

"Well?" he said in an impatient tone.

"Well what?" I snapped, and bit my tongue for being so rude.

"Are you getting anything?"

Oh my gosh! He wanted me to do a sort of psychic reading. I have never done those. I don't even know how I managed to acquire the ability to talk to ghosts in the first place. It started the day I met Rachel, after moving into what had been her apartment, and I have been badgered by them ever since. Sometimes, she even sent the darn things my way—her way of being helpful—but I think it was more her way of keeping my life interesting and herself entertained.

I looked at the corpse, but did not get any sort of message. It didn't work like that for me. Most of the time, the ghosts sought me out and always when it was most inconvenient. I stepped closer. One of the officers tried to stop me, but Detective Shorts waved him aside. He had a work belt tied around his waist, and a few gears, that must have gone to the clock, in his left hand, while his hair outlined his head in a mangled manner, possessing a slight curl. His eyes were closed, making it look like he had fallen asleep, except this was the permanent kind of slumber. I glanced around for any signs of the man's ghost hanging around, but saw only the park and the people from the police department. Despite my best efforts, I got nothing.

"I'm sorry," I said to Detective Shorts, "but I'm not getting anything."

His mouth formed a thin line and his face told me that he had predicted as much. I didn't think he expected me to get anything at all, but only called me here on the off-chance that I did. A part of me wished that I had gotten something so that I would feel useful and so that Detective Shorts wouldn't think that he had wasted his time asking me to come down.

"How did he die?" I asked, even though I had guessed the answer.

"Suffocation," replied the detective. "He had come here after the park had closed to repair the clock and it looks as though he was in there replacing a few gears when someone must have closed the door, locking him inside. Once sealed in there, it's like being in a vacuum. There is no air and the only thing you're breathing is what you exhale, so you suffocate in a matter of minutes. It doesn't take long."

"So, you think that he was murdered?"

"Until I have evidence to the contrary, I must treat this as a possible murder. Anytime a person dies under suspicious circumstances, it is investigated to rule out foul play."

"What was his name?"

"Jon Timer."

Timer? Really? What a fitting name for a clocksmith.

"I thank you for coming out this morning, Miss Summers," Detective Shorts said to me, ushering me out of the crime scene area.

"That's it?"

"I'm afraid so."

Disappointment covered my face and Detective Shorts must have seen it because he paused when we reached my car and leaned in close so no one else could here. "I called you out here because you have a knack for being contacted by... the otherworldly."

"You mean ghosts."

Detective Shorts frowned. "I thought if there was a chance of you learning anything that could help wrap this up, I would take it. But it may just be an accident."

I opened the door to my car and got in, turning on the engine and rolling the window down.

Detective Shorts leaned in the window. "I know it is pointless for me to try telling you this, but please stay out it. At least until we have an official cause of death."

"Always do," I smiled back at him and received a reproachful glare in response.

My phone buzzed and I glanced at it, noticing that

Jackie had sent a text. Detective Shorts walked away as I opened it.

Where are you?

Got a call from Detective Shorts asking me to meet him at the amusement park. Will fill you in on the details at work today, I replied back.

She sent me a grumpy emoji. ⚲

I left the amusement park, wondering why the clock-smith would be fixing a clock at night after the park had closed. True, there would not be a lot of people around, but wouldn't it have been easier to make the repairs in daylight?

Though the sun was all the way up, it was still early, too early to get to work, but I didn't feel like going home. Instead, I went to the edge of town where a wooded area was and decided to film some of it. I still had my camera in the trunk of my car after having to have it with me during this last semester for one of my classes. I pulled up on the side of the road, grabbed my camera out of my trunk, and walked out into the woods, following the unmarked trail, a path that many hikers had formed as they trekked through. I took my time filming the leaves on the tree as they waved in the wind and a bumblebee as it flew from one daisy to the next, collecting pollen to make its honey. I became so wrapped up in filming, and in just enjoying the serene area and some peacefulness that I do not often get, that I forgot all about the time and jumped when my phone buzzed from the alarm going off. Good thing I had remembered to set it. I turned off the alarm and hiked back to my car with a sigh. My peaceful moment had ended. Time to get back to the grindstone. The semester may be over, but I still needed to work in order to pay my bills. The joys of adulthood.

I received a text from Jackie. *Standing out here in the sun waiting on you.*

I chuckled. She was at least ten minutes early. *At least you can work on your tan*, I texted her back.

My phone buzzed as a new message arrived. *Ha. Ha.*

I texted her back, telling her that I would be there in a little while and locked my camera back in the trunk and drove off, heading back into the city on the backroads. Jackie waited in front of the door when I arrived and parked in the first, and nearest, space I could find. She tapped her wrist and smiled at me in her sarcastic way of reminding me that I was late… well… late by her standards.

"You're…"

"I'm right on time," I said.

Jackie cocked her head and arched an eyebrow.

"I was supposed to be here by eight and it is exactly eight o'clock."

"Congratulations. You can tell time. Now open the door. Mr. Stilton might be stopping by this morning and I don't want to be out here when he does."

"We should talk to him about giving you a key," I said as I unlocked the door and turned on the lights.

"Or we could just make a copy of yours."

"Wouldn't that be violating some sort of rule or something?"

"Only if he finds out," replied Jackie.

"I think you might be spending too much time with Tiny."

"Well, a girl has to do something when her best friend is off with her fiancé."

We put our purses in the backroom and each grabbed a box of candles to start setting up our beginning of summer display. Mr. Stilton had ordered some special citronella candles that were in these hand-crafted pots and wanted a display up before opening today, except Jackie and I were so tired when we closed two nights ago that we left without putting it up, deciding we could do that when we opened the store today. The only problem was: we had to get it done before he showed up with the money for the till, otherwise we would never hear the end of it. We spent the next hour setting up the table—I put a floral tablecloth down that I had gotten from the local dollar store—and placing the citronella candles on them. We stacked a few boxes in pyramids, and kept the extras under the table to replenish any that had been purchased, and Jackie had the idea of taking some out of their boxes and scattering them on the table in a whimsical pattern. I applauded her as it turned out to be a great idea. When we had finished, we stepped back and admired our handy work, only to be interrupted by an incessant and exuberant knock on the front door. We turned. Tammy stood there, banging on the glass with one hand and waving at us with the other as she jumped up and down, making her homemade, plaid capris jiggle as the tasseled weights she had on the ends bobbed in a frenzied manner. Did that girl have any fashion sense?

I moseyed over to the door and unlocked it, letting her in and taking two steps back as she charged inside in an excited manner, the tassels on her capris banging me in the calves. She trumped over to the counter, panting a bit as a few beads of sweat dripped down her temple (did she run here?) and dropped her crocheted purse on it with a thud. What did she have in there? Or did I even want to know?

"Did you hear?" Tammy asked, out of breath.

"Hear what?" Jackie demanded in a dry tone, but I think she had an idea of what Tammy was about to tell us because she looked in my direction and rolled her eyes.

"There was a murder!"

Oh boy. Here we go again. It seemed that every time someone died, Tammy assumed that it was a murder, or maybe she hoped it was.

"Murder?" I said.

"Yeah!" She flung her arms up and the bell-shaped sleeves of her shirt hit one of the citronella candles, knocking it over and would have started a domino effect if Jackie hadn't swooped in and caught the others as they started to wobble.

I helped her set them back up and she leaned over to whisper in my ear. "Please tell me that Cheryl didn't have an influence on her. I don't think I can handle another klutz."

I grimaced, sharing her feelings about having every little thing knocked over every few seconds. Back in April, we had decided to go to the circus while it was in town and a woman died, but her ghost had unfinished business and sought me out. The problem was, she, Cheryl, was a complete klutz. Whenever she turned around or tried to do something, she broke things.

"Yeah, a man was killed at the amusement park yesterday," Tammy continued.

Oh, great. She had already heard about the man who had died in the clock. "It was last night," I blurted out, whishing that I hadn't because now she knew that I had already heard her unexpected piece of news.

"You know?" Tammy's face fell.

I knew I should have kept my comments to myself. Tammy meant well, but her exuberant manner tended to rub people the wrong way, and always got on Jackie's nerves. Though, I wasn't sure if I should have been concerned about her tendency to get excited when she thought someone had been murdered. Maybe it was because she always looked on it as a chance to help solve the case, if you will.

I pulled out my phone and looked up the morning's local news. These days, it did not take long for the tragic news of someone's death to be posted online. Found it. I handed my phone to Tammy. "Sorry, but we had already read all about it."

She read the headline and the paragraph beneath it, along with the promise of more details to follow later and her disheartened look perked up a little bit. I think she just wanted to be the first to know something for a change and be able to inform everyone.

"So who do you think killed him?" she asked.

"I'm not so sure he was murdered," I replied.

"How can you be certain?"

"Well, not everyone who dies was murdered. It could have been a tragic accident," I told her.

I did not want to give away the fact that I had been called out to the amusement park earlier this morning and that that was how I had actually known about the poor man's demise. That would hurt Tammy's feelings. She wanted so much to be included in things.

"We shouldn't always jump to the conclusion that just because a person dies, that they were murdered," I said. "Sometimes, they do die of natural causes."

"But what if he was murdered?" Tammy asked in a low voice, thrusting my phone back into my hands.

"Then the police will—"

"Let you solve the case!" Tammy blurted out and Jackie rolled her eyes again while shaking her head, and probably biting her tongue to keep from saying anything.

"Mr. Stilton is here," said Jackie.

I shoved my phone into my pocket and hurried to the door to open it for him. He marched in with the bag of money in his hands, heading straight for the till and opened it without a word. We all watched as he placed the bills in it, counting them three times before he put them in their respective slots, and closed the drawer. "Morning," he finally said before going back into his office.

"Our ever present, absentee boss," Jackie muttered.

I flipped the sign hanging on the door so that it would inform people that we were open. When I turned back around, I noticed Tammy holding a handful of green tinsel and sprinkling it all over the citronella candles. "What are you doing?"

"Making it look more seasonal."

"Seasonal?" Jackie asked her in a dry tone, placing her

hands on her slender hips. "With what is normally used to decorate a Christmas tree?"

"Yeah. Now it looks like the candles are sitting in grass," Tammy said.

I heard a laugh, but could not find the source, so I assumed it had come from Jackie. "It's not that bad," I whispered to her.

"I didn't say anything," Jackie snapped back at me. "I sort of agree, but don't tell her that. It might feed her desire for more craziness."

I looked back at the doorway to the backroom, expecting to see Mr. Stilton there, but it was empty. Maybe I didn't hear a laugh after all. I glanced back at Tammy as she continued to sprinkle green tinsel all over the table, with most of it ending up on the floor. Did she just carry bags of that stuff with her? "Uh... Tammy, I think that's enough tinsel."

Tammy stopped and stared at me with a vacant expression. "Not even a little..."

I shook my head just as another snort sounded, and this time, I knew I heard something. I glared at Jackie again.

"What?" she mouthed at me.

"You keep laughing," I whispered to her.

"I'm not laughing," she hissed back at me.

"If it isn't you then..." Oh no. Why now?

Before I had a chance to even consider the possibility that we were not alone, Detective Shorts walked in and the door jingled as he closed it. Tammy almost squealed with glee when she saw him, having recognized him from the last time I had helped him solve a case, but Jackie's quick reflexes stopped her.

"Is there a problem?" Detective Shorts asked as he watched Jackie yank Tammy away with her hand over her mouth.

"No," I replied. I stole a quick glance at the door to the backroom where Mr. Stilton's office was, but he was nowhere to be seen.

Detective Shorts gave me a doubtful look, but did not press the matter.

"Is there something I can help you with?" I asked.

"Help? No." The detective pulled me aside, looking at both Tammy and Jackie, his demeanor telling me that he wanted to speak with me in private.

"We can go over here," I said, pointing towards the back room. I knew that Mr. Stilton was most likely in his office as that was where he spent most of his time. I sometimes wondered what he did in there. He never did run the store; that responsibility fell on Jackie and me. I led Detective Shorts to the backroom—and just like I suspected, the door to Mr. Stilton's office was sealed—and faced him, wondering why he had stopped by, since I had been unable to help him earlier this morning.

"I just dropped by to let you know that we have determined the cause of the man's death, the one whom we discovered this morning."

"And?"

"Accidental."

Accidental? He came all this way to tell me that? "Seriously?" I asked. The disappointment in my voice must have come through, because Detective Shorts frowned at me and gave me his version of the evil eye. I swear it could curdle cheese.

"You act like being murdered would be better," quipped a male voice.

I turned around, circling in place as I searched for the man who had spoken, but only Detective Shorts and I were in the room, while Jackie kept Tammy busy out in the main part of the store.

"Is there something wrong?" asked Detective Shorts.

"No."

"Liar," spat the same mysterious male voice.

Oh no. Why did he have to show up now? Why couldn't he have shown up when I was at the amusement park earlier, or not at all?

"So it was an accident?" I asked, hoping to get Detective Short's mind back on the reason why he had come to see me in the first place.

"Yes."

"How did you come to this conclusion so quickly?"

"One of custodians there happened to have seen us. After hearing about Mr. Timer's demise, he came up to one of the officers, asking to speak to me. He admits to having been cleaning the central square at the park last night and when he noticed the door to the clock sitting ajar, he closed it. It never occurred to him that someone would be inside and he admits to having been tired and not thinking to look in there as he wanted to finish up his tasks and go home."

"Really?"

"It was an innocent act and the man feels terrible about what had happened. Said that if he had known that the clocksmith was in there, then he never would have shut the door to the grandfather clock."

"Are you kidding me?" yelled the same male voice.

I could not take its interruptions anymore and lost my temper. "Will you shut up!"

Detective Shorts glared at me.

"Not you," I said, "but there is this… you don't hear him?"

"Hear what?"

"This man keeps interrupting us and…"

"I hear nothing."

Of course, he didn't hear anything.

"So then everything is finished as far as the investigation is concerned?" I asked, trying to get back on the subject.

"Yes, and you are not to get involved."

"Sure." I agreed, but the detective raised an eyebrow at my sudden willingness to do as he wished.

"I mean it. There is no murder here. The custodian's story checks out and I want to avoid another of your sleuthing expeditions."

"Avoid this!" screamed the disembodied male voice and Detective Shorts jerked his leg back as though he had just been kicked in the shin.

I looked at his shin before meeting his startled gaze with a surprised and innocent expression, while shaking my head and stammering, "It… it… it wasn't me!"

I do not know if the detective believed me or not, but he placed his foot back on the floor and walked out of the room, heading to the door before exiting the building. "I mean it," he told me before leaving. "No poking around. Just because I let you help last time does not mean that it was an open invitation for every time someone turns up dead."

"Oh, go find another body, you idiot. I'll find a real detective to solve my case," shouted the same voice.

I couldn't believe what I had just heard, and Detective Shorts must have heard it too because his expression soured and he shut the door with more force than usual.

"What was that all about?" asked Jackie.

I motioned for her to come over to me.

"What?" she said in a lower voice.

"I think we have a visitor," I whispered back to her.

"Visitor?" Jackie glared at me for a moment before her face lit up and she realized what I had meant. "You mean?"

I nodded my head.

"Now?"

I nodded again.

"Talk about great timing," Jackie retorted.

"Is that supposed to be a joke?" snapped the same male voice.

"Would you stop it?" I demanded of the ghost.

"Why should I?"

"Because it's rude!"

Jackie looked from me and the spot of air that I had been yelling at with a confused look on her face. I'm sure that she was trying to determine the nature of the conversation since she could only hear one side of it: my side.

"What's her problem?" demanded the ghost.

"You are!" I spat at him, before thinking through my response. The man was getting on my nerves with his attitude and refusal to show himself.

Something hard struck my shin, causing me to yell the word "ow" and grit my teeth as I held my leg and hopped in circles on one foot. "You little turd!"

I could only imagine what I must have looked like to Jackie, hopping around on one foot while I rubbed my shin and screamed at thin air, but she didn't run or say anything, having gotten used to these sorts of incidents by now.

"That hurts, you know!" I stopped jumping around and placed my other foot on the floor, still cringing from where I had been kicked.

"Making fun of my height now, are you?"

"Huh?" I said, confused.

"Don't play innocent with me," demanded the ghost. "You know exactly what—"

"I can't see you," I hissed.

"—I look... Oh."

Jackie and I both watched as a head appeared in mid-air that looked disproportionate and like it belonged to a larger body than the one it had. As a bit more of him materialized, I realized that the ghost was not a normal-sized man, but a little person, which might explain why he seemed to go for the shins.

"Aren't you kind of short?" asked Jackie, who no longer questioned when an otherworldly being showed itself.

"Aren't you kind of tall?" quipped the ghost.

"Don't get sassy with me, shrimpy!" snapped Jackie.

"OOOO, good one. Where'd you learn to speak English? I think you almost have a grasp of it," said the ghost.

"At least I can reach the top shelf."

"Isn't that underachieving for you?"

"Someone from the *Wizard of Oz* wants to know why you didn't show up for work."

"I got fired. And why are you squinting? It's cloudy outside."

"I hate clouds. And Frodo called. He says you're the worst friend ever."

"I no understand what you say," the ghost said, mocking someone who didn't speak English very well.

I just gaped at the two of them going at it with their verbal insults, seeing a side of Jackie I hadn't noticed before, though I had some difficulty not laughing at the sight of Jackie yelling at a floating head that talked back to her.

"You got a B on an exam once, didn't you?" continued the ghost.

"Aww, does your diaper need changing?" countered Jackie.

Okay. This had to stop. Someone could walk in on us at any second and I did not want—

A scream shattered the air and stopped Jackie's and the ghost's exchange of insults. We all turned and saw Tammy staring at us with a wide-eyed expression—and if her eyes got any bigger, I swear they would pop out of her head—as her mouth twitched in an effort to form another scream, which she did, before running off. This was just great. Now I have to try and explain to Tammy why there was a floating head in the Candle Shoppe. The thing is, I didn't know how I would clarify it to her because I needed the explanation to be one she would believe, as I did not want her to know that I could talk to ghosts, or have her spreading rumors about the Candle Shoppe being haunted. It was bad enough that she tried to tag along whenever I investigated another mystery.

"Who is that?" demanded the ghost.

"Tammy," Jackie and I both said with a groan.

"I better find her," I said, "before…"

"Jackie! Mel!"

Oh, crap. Mr. Stilton's irate voice meant that he had heard Tammy's scream and we were in trouble.

"Go see what he wants," said Jackie.

"What?"

"We'll figure something out. Just go." She shooed me out of the room and I hurried to the sounds of Mr. Stilton calling for us. When I found him, Tammy walked beside him muttering about hauntings and demons and who knows what else. My boss' expression indicated that he didn't believe anything she said and most likely thought that Jackie and I had played a cruel practical joke on her when we were supposed to be working.

"Mel!"

"Yes, sir?" I said, trying to keep my voice calm and hoping that Jackie and the ghost worked something out soon.

"What's this Tammy tells me about you two playing a trick on her?"

"Trick?"

Playing innocent was probably not the best way to go as Mr. Stilton's brows furrowed the moment I opened my mouth.

"It wasn't a trick," said Tammy. "There are ghosts here and—"

"I'm a very patient man, and have put up some of your antics for the past two years, but this is the last straw. I do not like games being played in my store."

"But, Mr. Stilton, we weren't…"

He charged past me, heading straight for the area where Jackie and the ghost were. The moment he turned the corner, I stopped and closed my eyes, afraid of what he would see and preparing myself for another outburst from Tammy.

"Mel," said Jackie in a disappointed tone, "you were supposed to stop them."

Huh? I opened my eyes. Somehow—and I'm not sure how—Jackie had managed to tie a string around the ghost's head, making it look like she had a puppet. The ghost looked none too pleased, but seemed to play along.

"What is going on here?" demanded my boss.

"It was supposed to be a surprise," said Jackie in a silky tone.

"What surprise?"

"Well, Mel, and I thought that we could do a little skit in the town talent show to help promote the Candle Shoppe. We were just practicing when Tammy walked in on us."

"Skit?" Mr. Stilton crossed his arm.

Talent show? Oh my goodness, I had forgotten all about that, but it was true that they were hosting one in a week at the amusement park.

"And the puppet you chose is that of a head?"

"It needs work," replied Jackie and I swear I saw the ghost make a frown, but he managed to remain silent. "We do apologize, Tammy. We didn't mean to scare you."

"This is not the place for such things," scolded Mr. Stilton. "Save this sort of thing for home where it belongs."

"Yes, sir," said Jackie and I together.

Mr. Stilton started to walk away, but paused, turning back around, saying, "When is it?"

"What?" I asked.

"When is your performance in this talent show?"

"They haven't told us yet," said Jackie, "but we'll let you know the moment we find out."

Yeah, they haven't told us because we haven't even signed up.

"See that you do. Back to work, all of you."

Jackie and I both breathed a sigh of relief when Mr. Stilton and Tammy left.

"Great," I said, "now we have to sign up for the talent show."

"Why?" demanded the ghost.

"Because now our boss is expecting us to be in it."

"Not my problem."

"You're not getting out of this so easy," I said.

"Hey, I'm not the one who lied."

"You're the reason we're in trouble."

"I'm not…"

"What if I help you," I said to him.

"What?"

"You must be here for some reason," I said. "If I help you with whatever it is you need in order to move on, then you have to help us with the talent show. And I never did get your name."

"Jon Timer."

"So, will you help us?" I asked, forcing him to give an answer.

"Deal," said the ghost. "Now get this string off me!"

"I don't know," mused Jackie. "I kind of like having a pocket dwarf."

They started to get into another bit of bantering, throwing insults back and forth at one another and I turned to leave them to it before a question popped into my mind.

"Why are you here?" I asked Jon. "The police ruled your death an accident?"

"Before I died, I heard two men talking."

"And that's important?" asked Jackie.

"They were plotting the murder of a third."

Chapter 3

What? Someone premeditated a murder and Jon over-heard? I needed to tell someone. I needed to tell Detective Shorts—Oh... wait a minute. He won't listen or believe me, not unless I have proof, which I did not possess.

"Do you know who the intended victim is?" I asked the ghost.

"No," replied Jon, "that's why I'm here. If I knew who it was, I wouldn't need you."

Ouch. Good way to strike me right where it hurts. "So, then, why did you choose to come to me?"

"I saw you at the park while the police were taking my... remains away. I thought it strange you would be there since you are not a cop, but then I heard that detective ask you if you got anything, or felt anything. I knew right then that you must be a medium."

"Thanks to Rachel," muttered Jackie.

"So I followed you. Now come on. We have a potential murder to uncover."

"Now wait a minute," I stopped Jon, "I can't just go running off. I have to work."

"Never stopped you before," grumbled Jackie.

"We're kind of on thin ice right the moment," I told her and she nodded in agreement. "I can't go anywhere until I can take my break."

Jon crossed his arms and a grumpy look crossed his face, reminding me of a toddler who gets disappointed when they do not get their way.

"I'm not risking my job for you," I told him.

"Fine," conceded Jon, "but when your break comes, then you are accompanying me to the park."

"Fair enough."

"Just one other thing," Jackie said, "do you think the next time he materializes, that perhaps we can have more than just a head. The whole floating and talking head thing is starting to creep me out."

"I'll see what I can do," quipped Jon, "my yellow friend."

I could not believe he just said that. Leave it to Jackie to not get insulted, though; she always let insults slide off her and ignored them, dishing it right back out.

"Well, you better do more than just try, shorty," she replied, holding her left hand out as though she was sizing him up. "What are you, like three feet tall?"

"Yeah? Well…"

I left the room, not bothering to find out what new insult Jon had for Jackie. They can just work it out on their own, though a part of me thought that they were having a little too much fun exchanging invectives.

Tammy glanced in my direction when I entered the main part of the store and walked away, no doubt still a bit frightened by the floating head incident. I didn't know if I should have been hurt or relieved that she avoided me. I decided to be grateful for it, knowing that at some point, she would quit being scared of me and insist on following me around.

I stopped when I noticed the display table that Jackie and I had set up earlier and almost screamed. What had been a beautiful display of our citronella candles in summer colors, had now been transformed into a mess of aerosol string, Christmas decorations, and confetti. Gold ornaments hung from the edges of the table, which wasn't so bad, except that more ornaments hung—and I don't know how she managed it—from the candles themselves. Aerosol string wormed its way around the candles, signs, and ornaments in a mishmash fashion, forming coils and braids, and falling off the table onto the floor, while sparkling confetti filled every crevice and the teeniest amount of space available on the table.

"Do you like it?" Tammy said, coming up from behind while wringing her hands together.

"Uh…"

"I think it makes it look more festive and the ornaments are the fireworks."

"July isn't for another couple of months."

"So?"

"Did you know that aerosol string is supposed to only be used outdoors?" I asked her.

"Oh, you can't always believe what the directions on the container tell you," Tammy waved away my concern with a flick of her wrist, causing her homemade charm bracelet the clink with each swing. Fuming over what she had done to the hard work Jackie and I had put in, I walked away. There was no point in scolding her. Tammy was Tammy, a person who possessed no control over her own impulses, being one to act first and think later, if at all.

The morning passed like most of them do: slowly. I watched as the minutes ticked by at their own leisure, forcing me to slump over the counter, wishing someone would walk inside, even if it was just to enjoy a little bit of air conditioned air before going back out into this unusual heat for May. Tammy pranced around, humming to herself, wrapped in her own world, as she fiddled with the candles on the shelves, causing them to sit crooked instead of straight, and twirling the charms on her bracelet. I worried about her sometimes. I hadn't seen Jackie. I think she and Jon were still going at it. At least she had a way to pass the time.

Growing bored, I pulled out my phone and cruised through my Facebook page, reading all of the posts by people who kept showing up on my newsfeed. Social media is a serious waste of time, but a great way to kill it when there is little else to do. I could only pretend to restock the shelves, or dust, so many times before even Mr. Stilton saw through my ruse. Though, I hadn't seen him exit his office since he yelled at Jackie and me earlier for scaring Tammy. I wonder if he spent his day watching videos on his phone while pretending to work. I know I would.

My phone chirped, informing me that it was noon. Finally! Now I could go on my break. It was only an hour long, but at least I could get out of this deadened place for a little while, though I had a feeling I would have company.

"Jackie, I'm going on my break!" I called to her as I rushed to the back room to grab my purse and car keys. "See you in an hour!"

"Bye!"

"You too, Tammy," I said as I passed the girl and her somber expression turned to a grin. For a moment, I wondered if she had any friends, or any social interaction outside of work.

I ran to my car and started the engine and had just pulled on to the road when—

"Leaving without me?"

Startled, I yanked the wheel and swerved a little, scaring the other drivers on the road. "Don't do that!" I snapped.

"You never told me that you were leaving—"

"Something tells me I didn't have to."

"—and I don't appreciate being left behind."

"Well, I don't appreciate having a ghost show up in my car unannounced while I'm driving."

A set of sirens sounded behind me while a set of blue and red flashing lights showed up in my rear view mirror. Great. Now I was going to get a ticket. I started to pull over.

"What are you doing?" demanded Jon.

"Pulling over," I replied.

"You can't do that!"

"I have to."

Jon reached over and grabbed the wheel, forcing me

back onto the road, while I tried to pull onto the shoulder. The car swerved and lurched as the two of us fought over the steering wheel and which direction the vehicle should go into. My stomach threatened to expel its contents as the car jerked to the left, to the right, before going to the left again, and I was thrown around in my seat.

"Will you let go?" I said through gritted teeth.

"We have a murder to prevent!"

"We can't do anything if I am in jail!" I screamed.

Jon let go just as I used all my strength to crank the wheel to the right and the car jumped over the sidewalk, onto the bike path, before slamming into a hedge that was against a stop sign. As I tried to catch my breath, the stop sign dropped from its post and crashed onto the hood of my car, causing me to jump.

Sirens bellowed as the police cruiser pulled up behind me, the flashing lights telling me that I was in a lot of trouble. I glanced at the passenger seat, but Jon had disappeared. Of course he was gone.

"Ma'am, please step out of the vehicle," said the officer.

I didn't budge, still trying to calm my nerves.

"I said, get out of the vehicle."

Sighing, I turned off the engine and stepped out, only to find myself face down on the hood of my car soon afterwards with my hands behind my back in zip ties. The officer gave me a Breathalyzer test, which turned up negative for driving under the influence. Once again, I found myself in the back of a police car (What was this, the third time?) and on my way to the police station. I guessed that my job would not be waiting for me when I returned.

"Do you want to tell why you were driving like that?" asked the officer.

"You wouldn't believe me if I told you," I replied in a glum tone.

The officer did not say anything else and continued onward.

We arrived at the station within minutes and the officer took me to a room where I was told to sit and forced to wait until I was processed. What a splendid way to spend my day. I don't know how long I waited for someone to come get me, but by the time I thought that I had been forgotten, Detective Shorts walked in.

"So now you are participating in reckless driving?"

I didn't say anything.

"You crashed into a stop sign."

"And a hedge." Jon had shown up.

"I had a little help with that," I said, ignoring Jon.

"Help?"

"Hey," said Jon, "I wasn't the one driving."

"But you're the reason I'm in this mess, you little twerp!" I snapped at the ghost. "If you had just let me pull over, we wouldn't be here. Didn't I tell you that I can't help you prevent a murder if I'm in jail?"

"Murder?" Detective Shorts' tone forced me to shut my mouth. "Do you want to tell me what is really going on?"

"It's not like you listened the first time numnuts," said Jon and by the way Detective Shorts looked around, I knew he had heard him.

If I could have put my face into my hands, I would have. "Remember when you asked me to come to the amusement park this morning?"

Detective Shorts nodded.

"Well, the dead man's ghost showed up after you had visited me at work."

"And the reason why you are here now?" asked the detective.

"Jon showed up unexpectedly in my car while I was on my lunch break and I jerked the wheel from being startled. That's when a cop showed up behind me. But he didn't want to pull over, so Jon decided to take the wheel."

Detective Shorts rubbed his chin. "You realize this is not going to hold up in court."

"Court?"

"You've been arrested for reckless driving and reckless endangerment, not to mention damage to public property. Honestly, Miss Summers, I don't know if there is anything I can do to help you and the 'ghost made me do it' defense won't work.

"Just great," I spat. "And I've probably just lost my job."

"I might be able to help you with that," said Detective Shorts. "In the meantime, you are being released, but you are expected to show up for court at nine in the morning on Friday."

Today was Tuesday. "And my car?"

"At the impound lot. You will have to pick it up, but I suggest you let someone else drive."

I followed Detective Shorts to the front desk, where I was signed out and we left the building without a word. He took me to his car, and I had half expected to be put in the back like the time he brought Jackie and me to his home to get rid of three little ghosts, but he opened the passenger side door for me instead. I didn't need an invitation to get in. The drive to the Candle Shoppe was silent and I went over what I would say to my boss when we arrived, but I was certain that I was fired. My phone buzzed and I looked at it for the first time since getting it back. Messages from both Jackie and Greg appeared, wondering where I was. I didn't reply. What would be the point? They would find out in the next few minutes what had happened.

Detective Shorts parked near the Candle Shoppe and I got out. So did he and he beat me to the door. I spotted Mr. Stilton through the glass, while Jackie and Tammy pretended to be busy, but both glanced in my direction.

"Mel," Mr. Stilton waved me over to him.

Grimacing, I approached, knowing what he would say. "Mr. Stilton, I—"

"Save it."

His harsh tone surprised me.

"Your break ended over two hours ago. You did not call, nor did you have permission to leave for the day. You're a good employee, Mel, when you're here, but the last year or two, you tend to take off unannounced. This is the last straw. I'm afraid I have to let you go."

"If I may interrupt," said Detective Shorts.

"Who do you think"—Mr. Stilton noticed Detective Shorts' badge and changed his tone—"um... what can I do for you, detective?"

"I am the reason that Miss Summers is late," replied Detective Shorts.

"You are?"

"Yes. She was at the amusement park yesterday with her friends. I'm certain that you have heard about the unfortunate man who was found dead there. I was here this morning to ask her if she had noticed anything unusual and told her to come find me if she remembered anything."

That wasn't the way I remembered it. Why was Detective Shorts covering for me?

"I do apologize if my wish to be thorough has caused her to be late for work, but that is my fault, not hers," continued Detective Shorts. "I'm certain that you wouldn't want to be responsible for impeding an investigation or would punish an employee for doing her civic duty. Word like that gets around and…"

Did Detective Shorts just threaten my employer?

Both Jackie and Tammy stopped what they were doing and watched every second of the exchange between Mr. Stilton and the detective. My boss turned toward them and they put their heads down, pretending to be busy working, but even a child could see through their ruse.

"I… um… well, no," replied Mr. Stilton. "Naturally, if she was assisting with a police investigation that is a different matter."

"So, I'm not fired?" I asked in a quiet and uncertain voice. Just how did Detective Shorts manage to turn this all around on my employer where if he had let me go he would look bad as it would soon get around town that he had fired an employee for helping the police in the investigation of a mysterious death?

"Of course not," said Mr. Stilton and Detective Shorts winked at me. "But in the future, inform me when you are going to the police station if it might result in you being late."

"Yes, sir."

"Back to work, all of you," Mr. Stilton said to Jackie, Tammy, and me before going back to his office.

"Thanks for that," I said to Detective Shorts.

"It's the least I could do for all the times you helped me."

"Yeah, but I could still go to jail for today's incident."

"I suggest you have Tiny contact that lawyer friend of his."

Detective Shorts said good-bye and left. For a moment, I thought I saw something move out of the corner of my eye, but when I took a closer look, there was nothing there.

I pulled out my phone to call Tiny, but remembered Jon's story about a murder plot. What if it was true? What if he had overheard something? A person's life could be in danger. I texted Greg instead.

Meet me at the Amusement Park at 5:30. Will fill you in on the details later.

He texted me back. *Will be there.*

Pleased that he didn't ask me for any details right then, I sent Tiny a text. *In some legal trouble. Need Calvin. Will be at your place later tonight to explain more.*

My phone buzzed with a reply. *Legal trouble?*

Will explain later, I texted back.

You better.

I smiled, knowing that Tiny would not let me get away without filling him in on the whole story, but that could wait until after I had a chance to search the plaza at the amusement park, which would have to wait until after I got off work. Now if I can just convince Jackie to give me a ride over there.

Chapter 4

It didn't take much to convince Jackie to drive me over to the amusement park. She was just as interested as I was in what Jon had told us. And where was he? I hadn't seen him since I was arrested for driving like a lunatic. I wondered if he felt guilty for getting me into trouble like that.

The sun made it appear as though it was only midafternoon when we entered the small amusement park, one of the advantages of it staying up longer. Greg waited for us by the entrance gate, tapping the heel of his foot. The feeling that he already knew about my little escapade washed over me, and whether he did or not, I knew I would have to tell him.

"Hey," I said as I walked up to him, giving him a kiss.

"I hope you have some money," he replied.

Money? Oh, what an idiot I am! In all of the commotion that had happened today, I had forgotten that we would have to purchase tickets to get inside. Good thing I carry a credit card with me at all times for emergencies, and this counted as one. I went to the ticket booth and pulled my wallet out of my purse. "May I have three season passes, please?"

"One hundred and eighty dollars," replied the bored attendant.

I handed her my credit card and she tapped her silver-green fingernail on a credit card reader that I had not noticed earlier. I swiped the plastic, pressed the okay button, and signed, bemoaning the fact that I was now $180 poorer. Oh, well. You do what you have to sometimes. She thrust the season passes at me and I took them, giving her the standard "thank you".

"Here you guys go," I said, handing Greg and Jackie each one.

"These are season passes," said Greg.

"Yes, I thought that perhaps they would be more cost effective than the single-day ones we had yesterday."

"How many times are you planning to come back here?" he asked me.

"As often as I have to," I replied.

"You're not telling me something."

"Remember the visitor I was telling you about a moment ago," said Jackie.

"The dead man's ghost showed up," I blurted out.

"That would be the visitor," whispered Jackie, rubbing her fingers over the sides of the park pass, which resembled a credit card and had its own chip on one end.

"And the cryptic message I got from Tiny about you needing a lawyer?" Greg asked me.

Dammit! I should have known Tiny would have called him, asking for more details. "Can we discuss that later?"

Greg folded his arms and glared at me, telling me that I would have no such luck. He wanted to know what had happened and he wanted to know now.

"I was on my way here during my lunch break when I got pulled over by the police and... arrested."

"Arrested?"

"Say good-bye to your perfect record," said a sarcastic voice. Jon had shown up.

"You know it was mostly your fault!" I shouted at him, garnering a few strange looks from people passing by.

"Starting to get the picture now," said Greg.

"Let's just say that I was fighting over the steering wheel with a ghost and I hit a stop sign which a police officer was none too pleased about. Of course, I'm the one who gets in trouble."

"Well, you were driving the car," said Jon, but only I heard him.

"You're the one who kept grabbing the steering wheel! If you had just let me pull over in the first place—"

"Okay, I'll admit that I might have had something to do with it," conceded Jon.

"Mel, do you think we can move this along because people are starting to stare," said Jackie, interrupting the exchange between Jon and I.

I glanced around the area in front of the gate and noticed that Jackie was right, people were staring at us and a few had gathered to see what was going on. "Let's go."

We went to the gate and swiped our passes on the card reader, listening to it chime as it read each one.

"Enjoy your stay," said the gate attendant in a monotone voice, probably wishing that the clock would tick by faster so that he could go home. I couldn't blame him. Some days are like that.

We hurried down the walkway to the plaza. Jon hadn't shown himself, but I had a feeling he was nearby, since he had insisted that we come investigate. When we reached the plaza with the grandfather clock in the center, I stopped, wondering how we would search the place with all of these people here: mothers giving their children something to drink, fathers carrying the kids on their shoulders, or the one child who cried regardless of what his parents tried to do to placate him. I didn't want to attract attention, but had to look for some clue that might tell us something about the conversation that Jon had overheard.

"We should split up," I said.

"What are we looking for?" asked Greg.

"You remember that Detective Shorts wanted me to come here this morning because someone was found dead, locked inside that grandfather clock?"

Greg nodded.

"Well, the man's ghost showed up while I was at work today. He insisted that he had overheard a conversation between two men, one where they were plotting to murder someone."

"Seriously?" Greg's eyes widened in surprise. "Does he know who they are or whom their intended victim is?"

"No," I replied, "before he could learn any more, one of the custodians found the door to the clock open and closed it, thinking that it had been left open by accident and scared the other two away in the process. I don't know if we'll find anything, but I don't know where else to start."

"All right," said Greg, "I'll take this end over here. Jackie you take that end, and you can search around here. We'll try to act casual."

I agreed and we all took our respective areas, trying our best to pretend that we were not searching for anything. I scoured the cement, not surprised when I found nothing but dried gum, discarded wrappers, plastic lids with their straws, and melted ice cream. What was I thinking? There was no way I would find anything in a crowded area like this.

"The voices seemed to come from this area," said Jon, remaining invisible.

"Where?"

"There," he replied. "Five feet in front of you."

I moseyed over, pretending to just be interested in some of the colorful statues they had there. A mother with her three children eyed me with a suspicious expression and I wondered if she had seen me walking in circles staring at the ground. I smiled at her and continued to study the statues as though I found them fascinating and pulled out my cell phone, putting it to my ear after turning the ringer off so it wouldn't go off while I pretended to talk to someone.

"Yes," I said into the receiver, "is there anything specific I should be searching for?"

"What are you…" Jon's confused voice told me that he couldn't figure out why I would pretend to talk on my phone when he was right there.

"It's a little loud here are you sure you heard them clearly?" I said, hoping he would get the hint.

"Oh, smart move," he said, understanding dawning on him. "I came here late at night when the park was closed. At that time, it is so quiet that you can hear someone coughing on the other end of the compound."

"Can you give me specifics about what was said?" I moved away from the statues when some parents gave me nasty looks for being in the way when they wanted to take a picture of their children standing next to the colorful pieces of art.

"Not too much," replied Jon. "The men seemed to be arguing over how to do what they wanted, though one seemed to want to back out."

"He didn't want to go through it anymore?"

"It seemed that way, but all I caught were bits and pieces of the conversation. It was the other man who seemed to want someone dead, like it was personal or something."

Personal? What could make a man want to murder another? A dozen reasons flooded my mind, but none of them made much sense, or helped me in any way. I needed more information, information that Jon seemed unable to provide.

"Do you know anything about the men?" I asked. "Is there any way you could have seen them?"

"I told you. I didn't see anything, I only heard them." The aggravation in Jon's voice came through and I backed off in my enquiring, reserving my inquiry for one more question.

"Can you remember, verbatim, phrases or words they used?"

Silence followed and since I could not see Jon

because he chose to remain invisible, I assumed that he was trying to remember. At least, I hoped that was what he was doing and that he hadn't left me. "Jon?" I prodded when he still hadn't responded.

"The only thing I can remember is that the one who was most insistent that they go through with it said, 'He's got to pay for what he did. Tony was family.'"

Family? That means that the one planning the murder had lost someone close to him, and had a score to settle. That was one clue, but it wasn't much to go on. If only I could find something else. As I wandered deep in thought, I spotted something glinting in the sunlight. No one else seemed to have noticed it. I hurried over to the shiny object and picked it up, holding it up close to get a good look at it. It was a button. Nothing exotic or interesting, but it did not appear to be made by a machine as the sides were a bit misshapen and not even. A small engraving filled the center of the button, and no department store button I knew of had such an indentation. Could it be custom made? Did they even make custom made buttons anymore and if so, where?

I pocketed the metal button, unsure if it would be useful or not, but it seemed to be an odd thing to find at an amusement park. Most of the people who strolled by wore jeans, shorts, t-shirts, tank tops, and if they had a button up shirt on, it was obviously store bought with solid colors, plastic buttons, nothing resembling what I had just scooped off the pavement.

Unable to find anything else, or get more information from Jon, I rounded up Jackie and Greg. They hadn't found anything interesting either, and our ability to search the place had become hindered with people ambling in every direction.

"Anything?" I asked them.

They both shook their heads.

"I'm hungry," said Jackie.

"Let's go," I sighed, disappointed that I had nothing to go on. I didn't know what to do or where to look next, and I still had to go to Tiny's, and I knew he would want to know the entire story as to why I needed Calvin's help.

Chapter 5

I arrived at work, having driven Jackie's car since mine was still in the impound lot, still half-asleep—I had spent over six hours at Tiny's the night before as he had wanted to know every detail of my accident— and wishing I could go back to bed, but knew that I couldn't. Jackie had the day off so that just left me and Tammy. Oh, joy. I gripped my travel mug of black coffee, having not bothered to put cream in it, which I regretted, since the cream masked the bitter taste, and stumbled into the Candle Shoppe. The unlocked door told me that Mr. Stilton was there already and didn't trust me to open up, not that I could blame him after my antics yesterday.

"Morning, Mel," sang Tammy in a cheery voice, her cockroach earrings swaying with each movement of her head. Cockroaches? Tammy has always had a strange sense of fashion, but why in the world would anyone wear earrings that looked like you had two dead cockroaches hanging from your head?

My wide-eyed expression and shocked face, must have informed Tammy that I had noticed her choice of jewelry. I tried to peel my gaze away from them, but my eyes seemed to be fixed on a permanent basis on the two swinging cockroaches.

"Do you like them?" she asked.

I took a sip of my coffee.

"They're not real cockroaches, just made to look like it," Tammy continued.

I took another sip of my coffee, still unable to blink away.

"My aunt made them. She is an etymologist, but also does beadwork on the side. I told her that I was looking for some unique jewelry and these arrived in the mail yesterday."

My eyes seemed to be glued open. I swore that the darn things actually stared back at me.

"So, do you like them?"

I sipped my coffee for the third time.

"Aren't you going to say anything?" Tammy asked with a child-like expression on her face, the kind where a kid might ask you if you like their stick figure drawing with their own Picasso flair to it and you said that you did, even though you thought it looked like every other kid's drawing, but you didn't want to hurt their feelings.

What did Tammy want me to say? The earrings are hideous? Why the hell does she have insects hanging from her ears? Is she insane? Don't answer that.

"Mel?"

"They're… interesting," I replied, unsure of what else to say.

Tammy either didn't notice my drawn out tone, or didn't care. She beamed and waltzed off to a shelf that needed straightening.

"Mel?" Mr. Stilton's voice caught me off guard and I cringed, afraid of what he would say to me.

"Yes, sir?" I replied.

"When you take your lunch break, you will be eating your lunch here today."

"I didn't bring…"

"You can get something from the café across the street, but I want you to stay here and away from trouble."

"Yes, sir," I said, perturbed at his insistence that I not leave the store, not that I could blame him after yesterday. I was lucky to still have a job.

"And, Tammy—AH!"

Tammy had walked up behind him and Mr. Stilton noticed the cockroach earrings for the first time.

"What are those hanging from your ears?" he asked.

"Earrings," said Tammy.

"If you say so." Mr. Stilton walked away, but Tammy stopped him.

"You wanted to see me?'

"Oh, yes, uh… you will be staying here on your break as well. For the moment, I think I will have to insist that my employees not leave for their break." He hurried away, no doubt wanting to get away from Tammy's strange taste in fashionable jewelry—not that I could blame him—and I heard the door to his office close.

Before I had a chance to do anything else, I noticed

a short shadow creeping across the floor and watched as the shadow transformed into Jon. At least, I assumed it was him, since I hadn't seen him in full-bodied form before. He carried a can of bug spray in his right hand, aiming it at Tammy's earrings. Knowing what he was about to do, I jumped for the can of bug spray, snatching it from his grasp, and he had a strong one for a spirit. He jerked it away from me, but I held onto it until I had managed to wrestle it from him. He let go.

Tammy faced me, having just noticed the commotion. "What are you doing?" she demanded.

"Nothing," I said, trying to hide the can of bug spray behind my back, but to no avail.

She peeked behind me and gasped. "Bug spray? Is that supposed to be a joke?"

"No!" I replied. "I saw a cockroach!" I could have kicked myself for that one. Really, Mel? You couldn't have thought of a different insect?

"Oh, and that's supposed to be funny?" Tammy crossed her arms.

"I'm serious," I said. "I thought I saw one."

I do not know if it was luck, the universe lending me a helping hand, or Jon having a bit of fun, but at that exact moment a real cockroach the size of my thumb and index finger put together scurried across the floor. Tammy screamed. She has earrings that look like cockroaches and that doesn't bother her, but she screams when she sees the real thing as it runs across her shoe? Good grief! I lunged for the insect, raising the can of bug spray and released a huge spray of misty liquid all over it, killing the thing in seconds.

Angry footsteps echoed from the backroom and I knew that Mr. Stilton was on his way to demand what we were doing. "What is going on here?" he shouted.

"I killed a cockroach," I said in a quick and tight voice.

"Mel, I don't—"

"No, really." I pointed at the dead insect on the floor with its legs curled up in the air, reminding me of a cartoon I had once seen.

Mr. Stilton sighed. "Great," he mumbled to himself. "Looks like I need to call an exterminator again."

Tammy's face paled.

"Good job," Mr. Stilton said to me as though he was congratulating a dog for performing a trick.

"You mean there could be more of them?" Tammy asked me when Mr. Stilton left.

"They tend to breed by the millions," said Jon, but Tammy didn't hear him.

"I wouldn't worry about it," I told Tammy. "We better make sure the door is unlocked and turn on the rest of the lights."

Tammy nodded and hurried off while I put the can of bug spray away.

"What were you doing?" I demanded of Jon.

"Getting rid of a pest problem, obviously," replied Jon.

"With bug spray? You could have harmed her!"

"The girl has insects dangling from her ears. If you ask me, she has no brains that can be damaged by an industrial product."

I did my best to give him what I always called "the mom stare", but he just glared back at me with his lower lip sticking out.

I stalked away from him, noticing that there was a

bare spot on one of the shelves and I hurried to the back, grabbing a box of our votive candles, making certain I got the summer collection set. When I returned to the votive section, I did not see Jon. Maybe he decided to bother someone else. I placed the new candles on the shelf, forming small pyramids with them, before breaking down the cardboard box and tossing it out the back door in the dumpster outside.

"You know, you need to quit delaying and help me figure out who is going to be murdered," said John when I closed the door that led into the alley.

"I have to work," I replied, in a low voice.

"You care more about your job than the life of some person?"

"When you put it like that—look, I'm in enough trouble as it is and I can't afford to lose my job." I glanced around to make sure Tammy and Mr. Stilton were not close by so that I wouldn't have to explain why I seemed to be talking to myself. "Unless you can remember something, some detail that will help, I have nothing to go on."

I heard the bell on the door to the store jingle as someone walked in and rushed out into the main area where I was supposed to be. One of our posters advertising some candle making class that a local resident was offering fell and I bent down to pick it up.

"If I had seen their faces I would have told you," said Jon as I hung the poster back on the wall. Something told me that he was the one who had knocked the poster down.

I didn't say anything to him, fearing that the woman who had entered the store would hear me, or Tammy, who happened to be putting her own spin on the tea light display.

One of the citronella candles shifted and dropped off the table.

"Will you stop it?" I hissed at Jon, who stood next to the citronella display with his arms crossed and his mouth set in a firm line. He had decided to make himself visible to me.

"You need to get out of here and start hunting for the two men I overheard talking the other night."

"I can't," I whispered, glancing around, hoping no one noticed me talking to the candles.

"More like you won't" grumbled Jon.

"I need more to go on. Would you recognize the voice if you heard it again?"

Jon's face softened and his eyes lit up. "Definitely. But how would I find him?"

I thought about that for a moment. This city was too big for him to just go around, eavesdropping on people in the hope of finding the one man he had overheard, but it was after dark when he had heard the two men plotting a murder. That meant that the park had been closed, so the two men were either employees, or they were trespassing, but why would you commit a crime just to plan a murder?

I wandered over to a secluded area in the shop, shielded from Tammy's inquisitive gaze and the woman who continued to meander through the store, and waved Jon over. "Go back to the park," I said.

"Why?"

"I think that perhaps the two men you had overheard might work there. Why else would they be there after closing time?"

"Good idea!" Jon ran through the store and out the

door, shoving it open with such force that the bell banged into the glass, releasing a terrible howl. Maybe I should remind him that as a ghost he doesn't need to use the doors, but can just pass through them, or disappear the way Rachel does.

I noticed the woman go to the cash register and I hurried over there to help her check out. She placed her two tea light candles, a duck-shaped candle holder, and three sticks of incense on the counter in a neat row.

"How are you today?" I asked in a polite voice.

"Just fine, dear," said the middle-aged woman. "I hadn't planned on buying anything, but you know how it goes sometimes."

I just smiled at the woman, having heard that statement almost every day, but I don't complain because customers coming in and purchasing items is what keeps me in a job, so long as I also manage to stay out of trouble. I rung up each item and wrapped the duck-shaped candle holder in some brown paper to protect it, and placed them all in a paper bag.

"That will be $twenty-eight dollars and thirty-eight cents," I told her.

She handed me two 20 dollar bills and I gave her back her change, handing her the bag with her purchases.

"You have a good day," I said.

The woman smiled and left without another word.

Well, that was one customer down for the day. I reached underneath the counter for the multipurpose cleaner to wipe down the table—it hadn't been cleaned in a few days—and noticed a rolled-up newspaper sitting there. Had the woman left it? I didn't remember her carrying a newspaper, but that didn't mean that she hadn't had one. I picked it up and prepared to throw it in the garbage when the headline on the page facing me caught my eye: *Man Dies in Burning House, Alcohol Involved.*

I unrolled the paper, my curiosity getting the better of me, and it wasn't as though I had any customers to take care of. A picture of the charred remains of the structure rested just below the headline with the body of the article next to it.

> Late last night, firefighters were called to the residence of 286 Ashtree Avenue in response to a fire. The small bungalow was already engulfed in flames by the time firefighters arrived. They managed to put out the blaze, but authorities have confirmed that the home's single resident, Henry Farford, was killed, dying of smoke inhalation.

> Henry Farford was well-known for his drinking. Neighbors recall that he routinely sat on his front porch with a beer and cigarette in his hand. Investigators believe that the fire was started by a lit cigarette that had fallen on the carpet. The blood alcohol level of Mr. Farford was 0.35 and it is assumed that he was passed out and unaware of the fire that his cigarette had started.

> "It's a tragedy," said Melanie Griffin, a neighbor of Mr. Farford's. "He was always nice, but he liked to drink."

Though authorities are confident in their initial assessment of what started the fire, an autopsy of the body will be performed, along with a pending investigation for possible arson.

That was too bad. What a sad way to go. I folded up the paper and dumped it in the trash can next to my foot, grabbed the multipurpose clearer and roll of paper towels, and wiped the counter. As I put the roll of paper towels and spray bottle of cleaner away, I realized that I hadn't seen Tammy in a while, which was unusual. Since no one else was in the store, aside from my employer, I decided to search for her.

I wandered over to the tea light candles where I had seen her last. No Tammy. Where was she? As I looked through a couple more aisles I heard a faint voice.

"Mel?"

I followed the whisper.

"Mel!"

The insistent voice snatched my attention and when I turned a corner, I covered my mouth to keep from roaring with laughter. Tammy stood in front of me, encased from head to toe in yellow ribbon, with streams of it sticking out of her pigtails in coiled bunches and blotches of glitter gel all over her face. I didn't know what to say, but Tammy's pleading look yanked the sympathy from me, though another part of me wanted to know how she managed to get herself in this situation.

"Help me, please!" begged Tammy.

Sighing, I walked over to her, placing my hands on

the back of her shoulders, and guided her to the bathroom. I hoped no one would decide that this was the perfect moment to come in and shop for candles. With an amount of tenderness that I didn't even know I possessed, I picked the silky stuff off Tammy and worked it free from her hair. She winced as some of it pulled, but I remained firm in getting her free of the entanglement she had found herself in.

"Do you want to tell me how you managed this?" I asked.

"I thought that the candles on the shelves needed some more pizzazz to show them off and I had an unopened package of this ribbon in my bag and cans of spray glitter gel... so I decided to use it as decoration."

I coughed in my efforts to suppress a laugh.

"You do realize that this stuff is supposed to be used as decoration and that you aren't supposed to wear it?"

"I just thought that the directions were more of a suggestion."

"So how is it you got this stuff all over yourself?"

"The thing got stuck and the stuff went everywhere and then this happened."

I pulled another stream of ribbon, dripping with glitter gel, from her curled hair. Yep. This sounded just like Tammy, and she was the only one I knew who could manage such a feat. Good thing Jackie wasn't here to see her. She would be posting pictures all over the internet, but I decided it was best to let Tammy keep what shred of dignity she had left.

"Next time," I said, "leave the can of spray glitter gel at home."

It took over an hour, but I managed to get Tammy free

of the ribbon and glitter gel and in all that time, I never heard the bell on the door ring or Mr. Stilton call for us. Thankful for that, I handed Tammy some paper towels and told her to clean her face while I brushed out her hair with my fingers to try and make her look less frazzled.

"Better?" I asked her.

"Thanks," Tammy replied.

"I'm going to go back out there and make sure no one walked in while we were gone," I told her.

I left Tammy in the bathroom and when she finally came out, I didn't see much of her the rest of the day. She must have been too embarrassed to risk looking me in the face. I didn't press her and decided it was best to let Tammy have her space since it remained quiet and dead the rest of the day. When closing time rolled around, I couldn't wait to lock the doors and get out of there, and neither could Tammy.

Chapter 6

The sun still sat high in the western sky when I locked the doors to the Candle Shoppe. Tammy left the first moment she could, still embarrassed by her episode, which I thought was odd because I had never known her to act humiliated. Maybe she just felt bad for needing help to disentangle herself from the ribbon and glitter gel. Mr. Stilton had left long before closing time, and neither Tammy, nor I, heard him leave, so he must have snuck out the back door, leaving me to finish locking up.

I pulled the key out of the hole when I heard the deadbolt snap into place. One final push against the door told me that it was secure and I turned to head to my car when a voice stopped me.

"Are you Mellow Summers?"

I faced the source of the voice. "Yes."

"My name is Leo and I wondered if I could have a moment of your time."

"This isn't a good time," I said.

"It won't take very long."

I glanced at my car, which wasn't parked very far away, wishing I could just go home, but the man's insistent tone forced me to stop and listen to what he had to say. "What can I do for you?"

He wrung his hands from nervousness, no doubt trying to come up with the right words. "I need you to... how can I put this? I need you to talk to Jon for me."

"Excuse me?" His request flabbergasted me. People do not just come up to me on the street, asking me to contact the dead.

"I wish you to talk to Jon for me."

"What makes you think I can do that?" I asked, keeping my guard up.

The man pulled out a crumpled newspaper with the library's stamp on, meaning that he took it from there, and showed me one of Jillian Mordsen's articles about my "fake" psychic abilities.

"Oh," I muttered. "I can't help you."

I walked away, not wanting to be ambushed by some of her followers, which had happened in the past.

"Please," he said, stepping in front of me. The despondent look on his face forced me to stop.

"I don't normally do these sorts of things," I said.

"I am not setting you up," said the man. "I do not know what happened between you and this reporter, but… I cannot go on, knowing that I am responsible for a man's death. I just want him to know that I'm sorry and that I hope he finds some peace."

Jon materialized next to me, but kept it so that only I saw him so as not to scare the poor man who looked as though he was about to breakdown any minute. He had a somber look on his face and, for the first time since I had met him, he kept his sarcastic remarks to himself.

"Something tells me that he knows," I said to the poor man in front of me.

"Are you certain?"

"Yes, and I think he forgives you."

The man pressed his lips together and started to walk away when a thought occurred to me.

"Did you know him?" I asked, stopping the man.

"Not very well," he replied.

Jon looked at me with a curious expression, probably wondering what I was up to.

"It's just," I did not know how to word what I wanted to say without it sounding so insensitive, so I just went for it, "you seem to be taking this really hard, more so than for someone who was not close to the deceased. I'm not trying to… I'm just saying…"

"I get what you are trying to say," said the man, cutting me off, for which I was thankful because my rambling reflected the jumbled thoughts in my head.

"Did you know him well?" I asked.

"Not well," said the man, "but a little. Jon was a transient, but a different sort of one. He had fallen on some hard times—lost his job and couldn't find a new one. He had travelled here in the hopes of finding some work, but there isn't a lot of permanent work to be had around here. It was soon after he had arrived here that I ran into him. We talked some. I help at the local soup kitchen and that was where I ran into him. Learned he was a clockmaker. Anyway, when the city decided to build their amusement park and I learned that there would be a great big grand-father clock there, I convinced Jon to apply for the job of fixing it. He was more than qualified and it would give him some much needed money."

"So that is why you feel so guilty for what happened to him," I said, realizing why the janitor took the passing of Jon so hard.

"I'm the reason why he was there in the first place. If I had known he was still in there… I should have checked, but I assumed he had come early to fix the clock and had left, but the door hadn't latched. That was his original plan."

"Something came up," Jon said to me.

"Something came up, forcing him to change his plans," I repeated to the man in front of me.

"I should have checked," the janitor said again.

"You cannot blame yourself." I placed a gentle hand on the man's shoulder, but did not know what else to do to comfort him. "He doesn't blame you."

"Thank you for that," said the janitor.

Before he left, I had a thought, and hoped he would be able to help, or provide some information. "Did, you, perhaps, see or hear anyone else there that night?"

"I don't remember seeing anyone," replied the man, "but I thought I heard a couple people talking when I was there."

"Are you sure you didn't see them?" I asked.

"I didn't get a good look at their faces. It was dark. All I saw were shapes and shadows."

"Were you able to hear anything they might have said?"

"I couldn't make out much."

That sounded familiar. I had a feeling that we would never figure out what had really happened or whom the mysterious men planned to murder.

"However," continued the janitor, "I do remember them talking about someone, someone they knew, who was in prison. From the way they talked, it sounded as though he had been there for a while… long enough to die there anyway."

"Die?"

"Yeah, it sounded like the person they discussed had died in prison and one of the men talking was really upset about it. Must have known him really well."

"Why would they be discussing this at the park," I mused to myself, but must have spoken loud enough for the janitor to hear me.

"One of them seemed to be wearing a park uniform," said the man.

"A park uniform?" I asked. "You mean that he worked for the park?"

"I would assume so."

That was interesting and explained why they were there at the park in the first place. If one worked there, then that would be a good place to meet. And if they both worked there…

"There is one thing that was odd," said the janitor and my ears perked up. "One of them mentioned making someone pay."

"Making someone pay?" I asked.

"Yes. I think his exact words were, 'He put him there. He will pay.'"

He put him there? Who put whom in prison? This was personal, then.

"Is there a reason why you are asking all of this?" asked the janitor.

I stared at him a moment, unsure of what to say. I couldn't just tell him that I was interested because Jon insisted that he had overheard someone planning to commit a murder and enlisted my help, or rather, wouldn't give me a moment of peace unless I helped him. "No reason," I said, though it sounded like a flimsy excuse, even to me and the doubtful expression on the janitor's face told me that he didn't believe me either.

He walked away, leaving me alone—Jon had disappeared again—but paused, turning back to me, still clutching that newspaper article that I detested. "I never believed the stuff she said about you. Not the bad stuff, anyway."

I didn't know what to say. Perplexed, and stunned that someone actually believed in me, despite Jillian's attempts to smear me earlier this year, I just stood on the sidewalk and watched as the man walked away. He tossed the crumpled newspaper in a nearby trashcan before crossing the street and hurrying away. I hoped he had found some solace in what I had told him.

Realizing the time, I hurried to Jackie's car, having borrowed it for the moment since mine was still in the impound lot, unlocked it, and got in. It was well past evening and Jackie was sure to be worried about me. I turned the key and pulled out, turning onto the road that would take me home just when the low fuel light turned on. Darn it! I knew I should have filled the tank earlier, but like a fool, I put it off, thinking that I could get a few more miles. Knowing that I would not get very far, I switched direction and took the road to the gas station we always used. Of course, this meant that I would be getting home even later, but it was better than running out of gas.

When I pulled into the gas station, only two other cars were there. It seemed unusual for it to be so empty on a nice evening like this, but I guess that even I get lucky sometimes and had managed to get there at a time when I would not have to wait in line. I lined my car up next to a pump and turned off the engine. After popping the gas tank open, I got out with my card and proceeded to pay and fill up the tank. My phone buzzed on the passenger seat. I leaned in the open window and picked it up.

Where are you? Came Jackie's insistent text.

Getting gas and something else happened. Will tell you when I get home.

My phone buzzed again. *Can you get some milk then on the way?*

Sure.

I turned off the screen and plopped my phone back on the passenger seat, making certain to touch the side of my car before handling the gas pump in order to discharge any static electricity that might have built up. It was an old habit I had and one that started when my granddad showed it to me when I was a kid and visiting him on Christmas Break. Static electricity gets really bad in the winter and he always touched the side of his truck before handling the gas pump. I remembered I had asked about it and he said that it was just a safety thing he did as it was a good way to get rid of any static charge you might have and prevent an unfortunate fire while filling up your vehicle. It's a habit I developed and still carried.

Once the pump had shut itself off and I had put it back in its holder, I took the receipt for the gas, grabbed my wallet from my purse, and went inside the convenience store that the gas station had. I did not like paying convenience store prices, but did not feel like making a separate stop just for some milk and I knew this place would have some.

The door jangled, giving more of a mechanical sound than the musical tone you would expect to hear, when I entered. The clerk looked up from his phone, no doubt playing that new game that was out, noticed I was alone, and went back to staring at his phone. Typical convenience store clerk. I didn't care. I knew where the milk was and only wanted the one item.

As usual, the milk was in the back, behind the chips, soda, juices, energy drinks, and beer. I wandered over to the single refrigerator that had milk, orange juice, some eggs, butter, and yogurt drinks. As my luck would have it, the gallon size containers of milk were out, except for a couple that seemed to have been opened and drunk from. Well, Jackie would just have to settle for the half gallon size, at least until one of us made it to the grocery store. I snatched a half-gallon of whole milk from the middle shelf and turned right into another shelf full of cookies. Of course, they would put the cookies next to the milk, as though I needed more temptation to ruin my diet, but one bag wouldn't hurt. I could go to the gym later, though that meant I would have to actually join a gym.

I snatched a bag of cookies, ramming it under my arm with the milk and hurried toward the check out before I found more stuff to buy. Something crashed on the floor in the aisle next to me and as I turned to see what had caused it, I noticed something that looked familiar: a button. This wasn't just any button, but was the same size, shape, and had the same engraving as the one I had found at the amusement park earlier when Greg, Jackie, and I had poked around looking for clues. Could it be the same? Could the one I had found belong to this person? I glanced from the sleeve button to where the head should have been, but a bag of chips and a baseball cap concealed the man's face.

He moved off. Had he noticed me staring at him? Still clutching my bag of cookies and half gallon of milk, I crept over to the next aisle and looked down it. No sign of him. Where had he gone? I spotted the baseball cap.

I moseyed down the aisle, pretending to be looking at the items on the shelf while trying to watch him, but not let him know I was observing him. I moved a little closer. The man glanced in my direction and I snatched two bags of chips, flipping them over to the side that had the ingredients list as though I was comparing the two. The fact that both bags were of the same brand did not help my ruse. I put one bag back on the shelf.

When he walked off, I tossed the second bag to the shelf, but it fell to the floor, forcing me to stop and pick it up, putting it where it belonged. The man had moved closer to the cash register. I slipped into the aisle next to where he was and meandered closer so that I would be right across from him, hoping to get a peek at his face. I took my time, somewhat, not wanting to spook the man or make him suspicious of me. As I drew closer, I tried peeking at him, but he managed to keep his face covered up, turning away from me some so that I did not get a full view of him. He had to have been on to me.

He looked up and I snatched the first thing my hand found, holding it up and pretending to be interested in it. When I saw what was written on the package, I almost gagged. Hemorrhoid cream? Of all the things to pick up, it had to be that. I would take anti-diarrhea medicine over that any day. I could just imagine what I looked like standing there, staring at this tube of medication for hemorrhoids while holding cookies and milk. Was that a smile on the man's face? I hoped he was one of the men I looked for just so I could call Detective Shorts on him.

I put the tube of hemorrhoid cream back in its slot on the shelf and moved closer until I was right across from the man. After making sure that he wasn't looking at me, I glanced up and almost got a full view of his face when his cell phone rang. Drat! I was so close. He turned away when he answered his phone and I missed my chance to get a look at his face and see who he was.

"Yeah?" he said when he answered.

I leaned in closer, hoping to get something, but was not so lucky.

"Will be right there." The man hung up his phone, dropped the items in his hands, and headed for the door.

Great! Now that he no longer carried anything that would require him to go to the cash register, I would not get a third chance to glimpse his face. I followed behind him, navigating the aisles so as not to look as though I pursued the man, trying to find something on him that could help me identify him, but his blue, buttoned up shirt and khaki pants were items bought in any clothing store.

He walked through the automatic doors, jumping into the car closest to the entrance and sped off. I rushed outside, squinting at the license plate, trying to get a number, but the sun had set and it was too dark to see the lettering. All I managed to make out was AX. The car itself looked like a Buick, an old one, but I couldn't be sure since I was never any good at identifying cars anyway, not the way Tiny and his gang were. There was some rust rot on the end of the right rear corner.

Discouraged, I puffed out a huge lung full of air and smacked my hands against the sides of my legs, realizing that I still carried the half gallon container of milk and package of cookies. I hoped the clerk didn't call the police on me to report a case of shoplifting. The last thing I needed was to end up back at the police station for another breakage of the law.

I hurried inside, running to the checkout counter with my items, while ripping out my wallet. The clerk had the phone to his ear and I had the sinking feeling that he had dialed the police. He hung up when he saw me stalking up to him like a madwoman. I threw the milk and cookies on the counter. The milk tipped over and, for a moment, I was afraid it might pop open, but I up-righted it and shoved it and the cookies at the clerk.

"How much?" I asked him.

Dumbfounded, or just wanting to be rid of me, the poor man rang up my two items, his piece of gum poking out between his chapped lips. "Six, forty-two," he told me.

I flung a five and two ones at him. "Keep the change," I said as I shoved another couple of ones into the tip box that sat in front of the cash register, hoping to placate the man for almost running off with two items of merchandise from the store.

I took the bag the man had placed my milk and cookies in and raced out to the car. I only slowed down when I realized there was no point in hurrying. The man I had seen was gone and I knew I would never catch up to him. As I sat behind the wheel of the car, I glanced at my phone, which still sat on the passenger seat. Three missed messages were on it: one from Jackie and two from Greg.

Before I had a chance to check them and see what they wanted, a resounding tap sounded on my window, startling me. I whipped my head to the side, ready to snap at the person who had disturbed me, but stopped the moment I saw Detective Shorts' face in the glass. I rolled down the window.

"Can I help you?" I asked, trying to sound innocent, as though I wasn't up to something, but he never believed me.

"What did you do?"

"Nothing."

He gave me that penetrating glare of his and I swore he already knew that I had almost walked out with two items from the convenience store without paying for them.

"I was just getting gas and a couple of things." I showed him the plastic bag with the milk carton and package of cookies.

The firm line of his lips meant that he mulled over the possibility that what I had said was the complete truth, or more likely a half-truth, as tended to be my custom around him.

"Is there something I can do for you?" I asked, jolting him out of his predisposition to ask me more questions.

"I stopped here for something and noticed your car."

"You mean Jackie's car. And I haven't been told I can't still drive," I said.

"A technicality which will be resolved by tomorrow."

Oh, darn it! I had forgotten that my hearing was tomorrow. After the way I had driven, even though most of it was Jon's fault, but you can't put a ghost on trial, much less blame him for everything.

"Is this why you stopped by to talk to me?"

"No," replied Detective Shorts, "I stopped you to let you know that your attorney has asked me to testify on your account as a way to help sway the hearing officer that you are not a menace to society."

My mouth went dry and my throat clenched up. Too many times I have gotten involved in a case that the detective was working on, and gotten into trouble, which he had to get me out of. "And?" I prodded.

"I'll be there," he said. "Whatever you do, you cannot let the hearing officer or the District Attorney—"

"The District Attorney?" I interrupted him. "Doesn't he have others who work for him who could try this case?"

"He does, but he remembers you from that incident with the blood in the hotel room and the nonexistent body."

I bet he was still fuming over the lost opportunity to put me in prison, and the fact that my Aunt Ethel slapped him so hard that it left a mark on his face for a week, which he passed off as a golfing accident.

"Do not let him know that you…"

"Talk to ghosts?"

"Exactly. I'm not completely certain I believe it myself."

"Do I need to remind you of the three girls, or Rachel? I could have her stop by for a visit, if you want."

"Please don't."

I almost laughed at his sudden refusal. When he had been in the hospital, Rachel took it upon herself to make sure he got well, and helped him eat by hiding the servings of meat on his plate until he ate all of his vegetables. I think she got on his nerves, but Rachel is not someone you just shove aside. She'll get even, as Jillian Mordsen can attest to.

"Just keep the communication with spirits thing to yourself," said Detective Shorts. "I'll be there to do what I can, but the rest is up to you and your attorney."

"Yes, detective," I said, knowing that he was right, and still angry at Jon for helping to put me in this situation in the first place. If he had just let me pull over to begin with, none of this would have happened.

Detective Shorts must have noticed my expression turn sour because his face turned to concern as he asked, "Are you all right?"

"Yeah, fine," I lied. There was no point in letting him know how I really felt about this whole going to court thing as there was nothing he could do about it.

He leaned in closer as though he wanted to tell me something that he did not want overheard. "This will all blow over. I know Tiny and I know Calvin. This is your first offense. I'm sure he'll be able to talk the hearing officer down. It's not like this is a murder trial."

I smiled at him, appreciating his concern and advice, just as a yellowed slip of paper spilled from his pocket with magazine cutout letters on it. I picked it up and unfolded it, reading it before Detective Shorts managed to snatch the note from my fingers and shove it back into his jacket pocket.

You're the reason for his suffering. You're the reason I lost him. You'll burn in hell and I'll arrange it.

"Is everything okay?" I asked him, concerned about the nature of the note.

"Everything is fine," Detective Shorts assured me.

I didn't like be shunted aside, nor did I appreciate having my concern about him dismissed the way you ignore a gum wrapper on the sidewalk.

"That was a death threat," I said, my voice stern and worried at the same time.

"Come here." Detective Shorts urged me out of the car and I followed him over to his own, ten-year-old sedan, with some of the paint peeling from the left side of the rear bumper. He opened up the trunk with his key, a small light came on as he did, and pulled a square, cardboard box, almost the size of a shoebox, out of the far corner of the trunk into the light where I could see it. He popped the top off, opening the box and stepped aside, beckoning me to look through them. I stuck my hand in and pulled one of the letters out, unfolding it, and holding it so that the dome light would illuminate the words.

It was a death threat. I picked up another. Same thing. I snatched a third and it had the same sort of message on it. After searching the box and looking at a dozen more of the letters, I realized that the entire box was filled with threatening notes, some of them quite abusive and full of language that I never thought people knew or used.

"What is all this?" I asked.

"This entire box is full of threats, most of them death threats, but threatening letters none the less."

"And you keep them in your trunk?" I did not know why anyone would want to keep such cruel thoughts directed at them in the trunk of their car. Why hang on to such negativity?

"I have another just like it at my office and a whole closet full at home."

I dropped the letters I still held in my hand, allowing them to scatter across the trunk bed. "Why?"

"I hang onto them in case I need them."

"Need them?"

"Miss Summers, in my line of work, receiving threats is part of the job. You cannot be a cop without making a few people mad."

"Some of those seem like more than just threats," I said.

"Most of them are just people mouthing off. They're all talk, but would never act upon what they say. The more serious ones are always investigated, but I keep them so that if something happens, the lead investigator has an idea of where to start looking."

"You mean, if someone takes a shot at you, then the lead detective investigating it has an already built suspect list."

"Precisely," said the detective. "I wouldn't worry about

it. Like I said, most of these are harmless. The ones foolish enough to put a return address on their envelopes are vetted out quickly and it usually turns out that they wrote it in the heat of anger, but would never act on it."

"And the others?"

"I wouldn't worry about it. Now, I think it's time you went home."

"I am capable of deciding for myself when I go home," I joked, but received a disapproving stare from him and realized that he was not making a suggestion or kidding. "I'm going home."

I got back in Jackie's car, still pondering over all the death threats I had seen in that one box in the detective's car, concerned that he had another in his office and a closet full at home. As a detective, he would have made plenty of arrests, testified at numerous trials, and helped put people in prison. Jon's statement about how the two people he had overheard talking referred to a man that was in prison who died, and how they wanted to get the one responsible, echoed through my head. Could Detective Shorts be the intended victim?

There was only one way to find out and I was going to need Jack's help on this one, though Greg would probably have to persuade him.

Oh, but I have my court date tomorrow! Finding out more information on who Detective Shorts could have angered would have to wait. For now, I needed to get home, shower, and go to bed so that I didn't look like a zombie in the courtroom.

Chapter 7

I tugged at my blouse for the fifteenth time since I sat down in my designated chair next to Calvin, the attorney whom Tiny had called when I had been arrested for murder and now was here helping me once again.

"Stop it!" hissed Jackie from behind. She and Greg sat together behind me, along with Tiny and his gang, giving me their support. I was certain that I was in for it this time and would end up in serving time in jail.

I clasped my hands and placed them on the table in front of me, wringing them so much that they turned white. I glanced at Calvin. His salmon-colored shirt and black suit coat accentuated well against his black skin, reflecting his calm and confident demeanor, something I wish I could imitate.

"All rise," said the Bailiff and we all rose to our feet, "Court is now in session with Lila Johanson as the presiding Hearing Officer."

A woman entered the room and took the seat behind the giant podium and those in the room sat only when she did.

"Bailiff, you may present the first case," said the Hearing Officer.

"The case of Mellow Summers. Charges are reckless driving, reckless endangerment, destruction of public property, and evading an officer," said the bailiff.

Great. I was in for it.

"Miss Summers, do you understand the charges brought before you today?" asked the Hearing Officer in a dry and official tone, as though she had asked this question over a million times from various people.

"Yes." I replied.

"You do realize that if this hearing determines you are guilty you can face a sentence of no less than five years of imprisonment?"

"Yes," I said.

"How do you plead?"

What was I to say? I could not tell her, the others sitting in the room waiting to have their cases heard, the bailiff, the security officers, or the transcriptionist that I was not guilty because a ghost forced me to do it. That would be a great way to wind up in a mental institution.

"Miss Summers?" pressed the Hearing Officer.

My lips refused to move. All eyes turned towards me, wondering why I stood frozen, unable to enter a simple plea of guilty or not guilty.

"Miss Summers, I am waiting." The annoyance in the Hearing Officer's voice rung in my ears.

"Not—"

"Ma'am, if I may?" said Calvin, interrupting me.

"Who are you?" demanded the Hearing Officer. "State your name for this hearing and your business here."

"Calvin Jeffers, ma'am, and I am here representing my client."

"You do realize that this is a simple hearing. She does not require legal counsel at this time."

"Yes, ma'am, I do, but according to habeas corpus, my client has a constitutional right to legal counsel whenever she is put on trial, and a simple hearing like this is still a trial of sorts as it will decide whether my client faces imprisonment, a fine, or nothing at all."

"Very well, you may proceed," said the Hearing Officer in a bored tone. I had the feeling that she had already decided on my guilt.

Calvin stepped forward, looking sharp in his pressed suit, cleared his throat, and spoke. "My client wishes to enter a plea of not guilty."

"Not guilty?" asked the District Attorney in an incredulous tone. "The officer's dash cam shows her car racing down the street and crashing into a stop sign!"

"Mr. District Attorney," said the Hearing Officer, "another outburst like that and I will have you escorted from this room. Is that understood?"

"Yes, ma'am."

"And, why are you here? One of your assistants could have handled this case."

"Ma'am," said the District Attorney, "Miss Summers was once a prime suspect in a murder case and I felt—"

"That has no bearing on this hearing. Unless you have proof that she did indeed endanger the lives of others, you have no business being here."

"If I may, ma'am," soothed the District Attorney, "I have the officer who performed the arrest here today to testify. I also have submitted the video footage from the dash cam of his patrol car, which shows Miss Summers evading a simple traffic stop, before driving over a sidewalk and crashing into a stop sign, thus proving that she is a menace to this society."

"And, yet," countered Calvin, "I have the sworn testimony of a well-respected police detective, saying that she has been instrumental in helping him solve impossible cases. He is also here today, ma'am, to testify on my client's behalf."

"Enough of this!" the Hearing Officer's aggravated tone silenced everyone in the room. "Bring a TV in, please, so that we may view the recording."

Within minutes a television was brought in with a DVD player and the disc showcasing my daring escapade was inserted. I cringed as I watched my car swerve from side to side before barreling over the sidewalk and slamming into the stop sign. I was done for. The evidence of my guilt was right there on the screen!

"What do you have to say to this?" asked the Hearing Officer of Calvin.

"Ma'am, I have a report here that proves that my client's car was not in good operating order at the time of the traffic stop."

"What!" yelled the District Attorney, but silenced himself when he noticed the glare he received from the Hearing Officer.

"The police made no examination of the car, nor did the prosecuting attorney, but I did call for a complete examination of my client's car to see if a mechanical issue could have been responsible for this."

"Bring the report here, please."

The bailiff took the report from Calvin and handed it to the Hearing Officer, who skimmed over it, flipping through the pages. "And do you collaborate with this assessment, Miss Summers?"

"What?" I said, without thinking.

Irritated, the Hearing Officer glanced at me over the edge of the report, saying, "Did your accelerator stick, thus causing you to drive over the speed limit, lose control of your car, and crash into a stop sign?"

Tiny started to say something, but Elise pinched his arm, forcing him to stop.

"Yes, ma'am." I said in a weak voice.

"So we can hear you."

"Yes, I agree with the assessment."

"Is the individual who performed the evaluation of the vehicle here today?"

"Yes, ma'am."

"Please stand."

A man I had never seen before rose from his seat and came to the podium I stood at.

"State your name," ordered the Hearing Officer.

"Joseph Sund."

"And is this your report of the vehicle's condition?"

"Yes, ma'am. Upon the request of the attorney, here, I performed a maintenance check and evaluation of the vehicle, finding that the accelerator had stuck, thus being the cause of the driver's inability to stop when an officer attempted to pull her over. It was mechanical error, not driver error."

"You may sit down."

The mechanic left the podium and took his seat in the audience again.

I didn't remember the accelerator sticking, unless you include the fact that Jon had shoved his foot on it. What was going on here?

"In light of this new evidence, I find the charges of reckless driving, reckless endangerment, destruction of public property, and evasion of an officer to be invalid and therefore shall be dropped. You are free to go, Miss Summers. But I suggest you get your car fixed."

Free to go? What just happened?

Calvin escorted me from the podium, out of the hearing room, and all the way outside to the steps that lead into the building where Greg, Jackie, Tiny and the others soon joined me.

"Congrats!" said Tiny, slapping me on the back and almost knocking me over. "I told you that Calvin would get you—that he would help you out."

"Hey," Greg hugged me, "at least this thing is over."

"Yeah, but," I said, "what I don't understand is how my car's accelerator was stuck."

"Hey, that's right," Tiny jumped in. "That car was in perfect working order. I checked it myself."

"Yes, well, sometimes things happen," said Calvin.

"Like a ghost fixing the car so that it would look like you had no control over it." Jon appeared next to me, but judging by the actions of the others, I must have been the only one who saw or heard him.

"I wouldn't worry about it," I said.

Tiny glanced at me with a questioning look on his face. I tried to let him know, without speaking, that Jon was here, but he didn't seem to understand.

"Yes, well," said Calvin, "if you all will excuse me. I have other cases to take care of."

"We should get going," I said. "I still need to get my car from the impound lot." I noticed Detective Shorts walk by on the far side of the steps, hurrying down them two at a time, and heading straight for his car. Remembering the threatening letters he had shown me the night before, and the fact that I hadn't gotten a chance to tell Jackie and Greg everything, I thought that this might be the time.

"I'll give you a ride over there," said Tiny, ignoring the glare he received from Greg.

Detective Shorts squirted past his car and hurried across the street, heading west at a fast-paced walk. Where was he going?

"Mel?"

His brisk demeanor conveyed that he did not wish to be bothered, but why wouldn't he just take his car? Could there be more to those threatening letters than he divulged? I don't like being left in the dark.

"Mel!"

I looked up at Tiny, not realizing that he had been trying to get my attention.

"Where's your head?" he asked me and I glanced at all the questioning faces staring back at me, including Jon's.

"Sorry," I apologized. "You were saying, Tiny?"

"Nah-uh," said Tiny. "You're not getting away with it this easily. You should be celebrating that the charges were dropped, but your mind seems to be somewhere else. What gives?"

"Maybe, we shouldn't discuss that here," I said.

"My place. Two hours," said Tiny.

Greg looked as though he wanted to object, but the look on Tiny's face ended any such thoughts.

"All right," I agreed, knowing I was not going to get out of it. Besides, it would give me the time I needed to get my car.

Chapter 8

Greg drove me to the impound lot to get my car while Jackie went with Tiny and his gang to his place. At first, she wasn't going to, but he promised her chili dogs so she changed her mind. The impound lot lay more in the center of the city, or what was once considered the very center until businesses and subdivisions rose up around it, making it more to the left of center, but it was downtown none-the-less. The ride was quiet, for the most part, but I could tell that Greg debated asking me to explain my comments from earlier, or to just let it slide. His more curious side won out, though, because about halfway to the impound lot he quit chewing on the corner of his lip and asked, "So, what is this all about?"

"What?" I replied.

"Your sudden worry about Detective Shorts."

"It's probably nothing," I said.

A snort came from the backseat.

I turned around in my chair, straining the seatbelt to the point where it threatened to pull away from its hold. "Will you quit doing that?"

"Doing what?" demanded Jon.

"Laughing like that whenever someone says something that you don't agree with or like," I snapped at him.

"Then, quit saying things that sound stupid!"

"Stupid!" I almost crawled into the backseat, wanting to slap him, but remembered that you can't hit a ghost.

"Mel, will you get back in your seat?" said Greg, a little worried about me getting angry at something he couldn't see.

I stopped trying to get at Jon and settled back into that passenger seat, mumbling, "Sorry."

"Well, you should be," said Jon.

I clenched my fists.

"It's okay," soothed Greg, noticing my rising anger. I did not know if he heard Jon or not, but breathed in a deep lung-full of air, calming myself and unclenched my fists.

"You can be really annoying sometimes," I said to Jon.

"You are not the first one to tell me that," he replied.

Big surprise there. I just wanted him to stop with the snorting and the laughing... and the kicking of shins. "Do you think you could try to be a bit more respectful?" I asked him.

Silence followed for a moment before he answered. "I will try not to laugh at things that I think sound... unreasonable."

Well, that was an improvement.

"What makes you think that this Detective Shorts guy might be in danger?" asked Jon.

"Didn't you see the box of threats he has received over the years?"

"Uh…no. I wasn't with you last night when that happened."

"Not to be rude," said Greg, while still driving the car "but do you two—I assume that we are not alone—mind including me in your conversation?"

"Well, excuse me," said Jon, appearing in the back seat, and judging by Greg's surprised look, he must have watched him materialize out of thin air.

"That's better," muttered Greg, taking several glances into the rear-view mirror to make sure that Jon wasn't some sort of optical illusion.

"So you say this detective has gotten death threats?" asked Jon.

"Yes, I replied. "When I was at the gas station last night, I ran into Detective Shorts. He showed me a box full of threats that he has received and he said that he has more in his office and at his house. Some of them were benign, but others got downright nasty to where they actually promised to put him in his grave."

"That's a start," said Jon.

"Why am I just now hearing about this?" Greg asked me.

"I'm sorry," I apologized to him. "I meant to tell you and Jackie when I got home last night, but it was so late and I had other things on my mind. Forgive me?"

"Forgiven," said Greg.

"Thanks," I replied with a wan smile.

"Oh mush!" Jon snorted. "Get a room you two."

"There was something else too," I said.

"Oh," Greg and Jon said together.

"When I stopped for gas, I went into the convenience store to get something and I saw a man wearing a shirt with the same type of buttons like the one I had found at the carnival."

"Are you sure they were the same?" Greg asked.

"They looked very similar but it's not like I was able to compare the two side by side."

"Who cares about that!" shouted Jon. "Did you see the man's face?"

My face fell. "No."

"Well, that puts us right back where we were," huffed Jon, crossing his little arms and giving me a pouty face, which I don't think he realized he was doing.

"Not quite," I said. "I got a partial license plate number."

"We're here," said Greg, turning into the impound lot and parking in front of the small, shack-like building where the attendant was. "You said you got a partial license plate number?" he asked me before I got out of the car.

"Yeah."

"Write it down for me and I'll give Jack a call." Greg handed me his phone, with the notepad app open and I wrote down the two letters that I managed to decipher. He gave me a questioning look. "That's it?"

"It was really dark," I replied.

"I'll send this to Jack and see if he gets anything. Maybe I can have him look up some of Detective Shorts' old cases, too."

"Good luck," I said, giving him a peck on the cheek, knowing how Jack would react to this latest request of ours.

Though, I think he secretly liked helping us investigate things, but always put on a show of not wanting to be bothered.

I stepped out of the car, looking around for Jon, but didn't see him so he must have decided to wander off, or at least go back to being invisible. I walked up to the small building and the shatter proof glass that separated me and the attendant, who glanced up in my direction from the game he played on his phone, but still did not bother to acknowledge my presence.

"Excuse me?" I said.

"Yeah," came his coarse reply as he continued to tap the screen of his phone while chewing on an unlit cigar. I guess his game was more important than doing his job.

"I'm here to pick up my car," I said.

"Uh-huh," he muttered, still paying more attention to his game than to me.

Growing frustrated, and sick and tired of people treating me as though I was just a piece of gum stuck on their shoe, I slammed my fist against the shatterproof glass, yelling, "Hey! Give me my car right now!"

The man put his phone down and stood up, rising to his full height, making me wish that I had Tiny with me, or that I had acted more pleasant instead of trying to throw my weight around. "Maybe, I'm busy and maybe, I can't find your car."

I gawked at him, unsure of what to do. "Just give me the paperwork to sign, the keys, and I'll be on my way."

The attendant did not budge and I regretted my little outburst.

"You know"—Jon appeared next to the man, leaning on the small counter that was inside the tiny building and looked at me—"you really need to learn to control those anger issues of yours. Didn't anyone ever tell you that you attract more flies with honey?"

"She might have mentioned something similar," I said, unsure of what Jon was up to.

The cigar dropped from the man's mouth as he gaped at Jon, the fear growing on his face.

Jon turned toward him. "What? Haven't you ever seen a dwarf before?"

"You just referred to yourself as a dwarf, but got all angry when Jackie did the same thing," I said to him.

"It's not offensive when I say it," countered Jon.

"Oh, what a bunch of bull—"

"Hey," Jon interrupted me, "we have more important things to do right now than argue." He faced the attendant again. "Look, pal, we have a murder to prevent and killers to catch, so give her the keys to her car right now. We're running out of time here."

The man charged out of the small shack, pulling his pants up (they kept falling down) as he did so.

"Typical," muttered Jon. "You'd think he'd never seen a little person before."

Frustrated at still not having the keys to my car, I walked around to the door and entered the shack, looking through the file drawers and the hooks on the wall that held keys with small stickers attached to them, each with a number.

"I think his behavior has more to do with you being a ghost, than with your short stature," I said to Jon.

I woke up the computer and opened a file marked "inventory". It was a place to start. As I scrolled through it, I realized that I had guessed right and scanned each name on there, driver's license number, and the car that was attached to the name, looking for my own. Found it! According to the record, my key was numbered 22 and my car was on the south end of the lot in Section D. I scanned the keys hanging from their hooks, finding mine with a tag labeled 22 attached to it, snatched it from the wall, and hurried outside.

It took a few minutes, but I managed to locate Section D of the impound, stopping when I saw my car. What had once been a clean and polished vehicle had morphed into a piece of metal coated in an inch of dust. A dent rested on the front bumper, which I know had not been there when my car had been impounded. I walked around my vehicle, cursing as I looked at each nick and chip in the paint. What did they do to my car in the few days they had it? Take it to a demolition derby?

Fuming, I rammed the key into the lock and opened the driver's door, wincing as it creaked, reminding me of an old station wagon that my grandmother used to drive. Had my car aged 30 years in the last 48 hours? Tiny would not be thrilled by this, and considering that I wasn't happy, I knew that he would have a few choice words. The engine had better start.

I plopped down in the driver's seat and swore as a cloud of dust burst out of the open door, doing my best not to cough. Holding my breath, I put the key in the ignition and turned, pleased that it started without a hitch. I slammed the door shut and turned on the wipers to clean some of the dust off the windshield, but only managed to create huge, black streaks.

"Wow," said Jon, appearing in the passenger seat, "what a wreck."

I glared at him. "It wasn't like this the day it was impounded and you know it."

"You're never going to get over the fact that you were arrested, will you?"

Was he serious? He knew full well, what had happened! I felt my cheeks turn red as the anger rose within me and would have chewed him out, if he hadn't glanced in my direction and mumbled a soft "Sorry" after seeing my face.

"Can we go now?" he asked in a bored tone, much like the way a child asks their parents.

I put my car in drive and steered my way towards the entrance gate where Greg waited for me. He leaned against the hood of his car with his phone to his ear—most likely talking to Jack—but paused when he saw my car. I watched as he straightened up and lowered his phone a little, his jaw dropping at the terrible state of my car. I pulled up beside him.

"Huh—yeah!" he said back in his phone, indicating that Jack must have been yelling at him to get his attention. "I need you to look up… No, I don't always… Now, Jack… Will you shut up a minute? I need you to try and figure out where those two numbers go to.… Yes, I know that it is only the first two digits of a license plate number, but that doesn't mean you won't find something."

Greg glanced at me and I wondered how long he had been negotiating with Jack as it sounded like Jack had become impervious to his charms. "Don't you want to help prevent a possible murder?"

Silence followed and judging by the way Greg held his phone away from his ear, Jack must have been screaming at him. I think I even heard a few uncivilized phrases myself.

"She thinks it might be Detective Shorts… Well, he is a detective and… Come on, Jack, you know we need your help."

"Hell no!" came Jack's voice through Greg's phone and I was surprised that even I heard that response clearly.

"Okay, Jack, have it your way," said Greg. "You know, your mother has been wanting to come down for a visit and I happen to have a spare bedroom. I was thinking of…"

I watched as a devilish smile crept across Greg's face. He always knew how to convince Jack to do something.

"I thought you would understand," said Greg and he hung up.

"Your boyfriend is quite the extortionist," commented Jon.

I smiled. I guess he was, but it always helped us when we were trying to figure out a mystery.

"He'll do it," Greg said to me, putting his phone back into his pocket. "Uh, what happened to your car?"

The irate look on my face must have convinced him to not go any further since he clamped his mouth shut and got back into his own car. "See you at Tiny's."

I followed Greg over to Tiny's and we arrived there in about 35 minutes. Tiny waited for us at the entrance to his garage, with his arms folded, and his jaw tightened when he saw the current state of my car. How would I explain this to him? I parked just outside and turned off the engine. When I got out of the car, Tiny had already hurried over, investigating the new dent and the chipped paint and cringing when he heard the squeak in the driver's door hinges.

"What did they do to your car?" he demanded.

I shrugged my shoulders. How should I know? I was just as incensed about this as he was. Ever since we became friends, Tiny has insisted on maintaining my car—he and his gang fixed cars for a living and he owned his own garage—and he took pride in his handiwork. So, whenever he saw my car, or any vehicle that he serviced, looking like a wreck, he took it as a personal insult. "It wasn't like this when they impounded it."

"Someone's going to get a call from me," Tiny muttered to himself as he propped the hood up and looked at the engine. "There's even dust in here. This is going to take some time to fix."

"Not to be rude, or anything," said Jon, materializing beside Tiny, "but we do have a potential murder to solve."

Tiny jumped back with a start and Jon disappeared, surprised by Tiny's reaction. "You... uh... you need to warn me when one of your friends are here."

"They don't always warn me," I said, going inside to where Jackie and Greg waited, followed by Tiny who must have thought it best to agree with the ghost, rather than anger an otherworldly being.

"So," said Tiny to me, after we all sat down, "I think it is time you started explaining a few things."

Where do I begin? "It started earlier this week when Detective Shorts called me to commune with the spirit of a dead man, the one found in the grandfather clock at the amusement park."

For the next half hour, I explained to them how Jon had shown up at the Candle Shoppe, my escapade with the police officer that had tried to pull me over, and Jon's insistence that he had overheard a possible plot by two people to commit murder, except we didn't know who the intended victim was.

"And you believe the target might be the detective?" asked one of Tiny's friends.

"It makes sense," I said. "He showed me the threats he receives on a daily basis."

"But it could be anyone," reminded Tiny.

"True," I said, "but at this point, we don't have much to go on."

"Is there anything else he could tell us?" asked Tiny. "He… uh… made his presence known earlier. Couldn't he do it again?"

Jackie piped in. "He's a little shy because he needs a step ladder to reach the couch." When Tiny gave her an inquiring look, she used her hands to illustrate how short he was.

"You know, cosmetic surgery is quite good these days and could help open those slanted eyes of yours!"

I could have smacked the pair of them. I looked around for Jon, but saw no sign of him as he remained invisible, but judging by the look on Jackie's face, and what she said next, I know she had heard him.

"Gimli says you need to grow a bit before he'll let you borrow his axe."

"Immigration called," said Jon, still remaining invisible, "they want to see your papers."

"Oh my gosh, you two," I said to them. "Stop it!"

I glanced around the room and at the curious faces before me. They must have heard him. I know they heard him.

"So this Jon fellow is a short guy?" asked Tiny, trying to find the politest way to ask if he was a midget.

"Hey, I may be short," said Jon, "but I make up for it in other ways, if you know what I mean."

I did not need to know that. I tried to slap him out of annoyance, but ended up hitting thin air instead.

"Can we focus our attention back to the fact that a man's life is in danger?" asked Greg.

"So, you think it's Detective Shorts," said Tiny again.

"Right now, yes," I replied. "Unless we get something else that points us in another direction. Plus, he acted weird when he left the courthouse this morning."

"Weird?" asked Jackie.

"I watched him as he walked past his car and across the street, hurrying down the sidewalk as though he did not want to be followed. Why would he walk where he wanted to go when he had his car right there?"

"It is possible," Greg replied, "that he was going someplace nearby."

That was true, but something about the way he walked, looking around to make sure he wasn't being followed, made me think that there was more to it. "Possibly," I conceded, "but can we rule him out just now?"

The people around me shook their heads. As a detective, he would garner enemies. Jon himself mentioned that one of the men he had overheard wanted the person who had wronged him to pay. If it was someone Detective Shorts had arrested in the past, it stands to reason that he would be the intended target. At the very least, I had to know more in order to confirm whether he was or wasn't on the mysterious men's list.

"What do you want to do?" asked Greg.

Before I had a chance to answer Jackie blurted out, "Tail him!"

"What?" asked Greg.

"We will follow him around town," replied Jackie. "Perhaps we'll learn where he was going when you saw him this morning, Mel, and we might learn whether he is our unannounced victim."

"What a dumb…" began Jon.

"And our resident ghost can help," said Jackie, "unless, of course, he feels he doesn't measure up to the job."

I gaped at her and her brazen insult, but she just winked at me.

"I'll show you all I can do it," said Jon, loud enough that everyone in the room heard him. "You just tell me when you want me to tail him."

"How about right now?" I said. "At least, you can tell us where he is and we'll pick it up from there."

Jon disappeared.

"All right, fellas," said Tiny to his men, "let's go! No time like the present."

Chapter  9

I sat in my car waiting for a call from Tiny, hoping that no one noticed me just sitting on the side of the road. For the most part, I went unnoticed as cars sped past, oblivious, or not caring, that I had been parked on the shoulder for the last half hour, though some drivers did give me rude glances for being in their way, forgetting that they are not supposed to drive on the shoulder in the first place.

I checked my phone, having downloaded an app that would read text messages for me, and allow me to speak to it, turning my words into an actual text message that can be sent. It's almost like having a real walkie talkie. No messages. How much longer would I have to sit here?

In answer to my question, my phone chirped.

Message from Tiny. The cop is on his way. Will switch off in five.

I started the engine. More cars whizzed past me. I checked the clock in my car. It's been almost five minutes. At any moment Detective Shorts should—

His car appeared, turning from a side street onto the road I was on. I waited a few seconds as he drove away before veering into traffic and watched as Tiny pulled off, continuing down another road. Two cars placed themselves between me and the detective, but I maintained my pace and kept him in sight, thankful that my car was coated in grime, making it unrecognizable. He changed lanes. I followed suit. He moved into the left turn lane and I maneuvered over as well, making the turn just as the light changed yellow. I switched to the right lane while he stayed in the left, not wanting to give away the fact that I followed him.

"Send text to all contacts in friends folder," I said to the app on my phone. "Just turned onto Applewood, heading towards the mall. If I keep following, he'll get suspicious."

My phone chirped, informing me that my message was sent. Another chirp sounded and I tapped the screen to open it.

Keep on him until you get to Carver Street. Will take over from there.

I turned off onto Carver Street and watched in my rearview mirror as Greg pulled out onto Applewood. So far, so good. I found an open parking lot and steered my car into it, finding a space that was away from those trying to park closest to the door of the department store.

My phone chirped and I tapped the screen again to open the message from Greg.

Stopped at a Starbucks. Tiny, can one of you pick up?

I started my car and headed for where Greg was.

Another chirp brought my phone to life.

Sticky will be on him from there.

I continued to listen to the messages that spilled in on my phone as we switched off, while starting my car again and maneuvering through the city on the back-roads, ready to pick up where another left off if needed. After Sticky had trailed Detective Shorts for a couple of miles, he stopped, allowing Jackie to pick up the tail.

Going towards Mason's Furniture Store.

Following her text, I turned, taking the most direct route to Mason's Furniture Store.

Another message from her came through. *He stopped at a hot dog stand on corner of Wilmar and North. Am turning off now.*

My phone chirped again.

Sombrero picking up.

I headed for Wilmar and North. So far, Detective Shorts hadn't gone anywhere that would help us learn if he was in danger or not. This started to turn into a dead end. If nothing happened soon, I was going to call it off. As I listened to the messages spilling through my phone, I learned that Detective Shorts stopped at a pawn shop and talked to the owner there before swinging past a convenience store to pick up two sodas; all the while, Tiny's friends switched off, each taking their turn in following him so that he would not know he was being shadowed.

As I continued tracking their accounts of where he went, I bypassed him on the road. I hoped he didn't recognize me. My phone chirped and a message from Greg came through, as it was his turn to follow him again.

He is turning back around onto Applewood.

Where was he going? I wondered? I headed for Apple-wood. "Send message to friends folder," I told my phone. "Am taking over for now."

My phone chirped, letting me know that it had sent the message to everyone.

I drove down Applewood once again, but saw no sign of Detective Shorts' car. Had he taken another road before I had a chance to spot him? I tapped my phone's screen and was about to send another message to everyone when a pair of sirens whooped behind me. Glancing in my rearview mirror, I realized that Detective Shorts was right behind me. Sighing, I pulled over, knowing that the ruse was up. Within moments of me pulling onto the shoulder and shutting my car off, a tap rattled my window.

"Miss Summers," said Detective Shorts.

"Hi," I replied in an innocent voice.

He handed me a hot dog and a cola.

"What's this for?" I asked, but my playing coy was getting me nowhere, and his arched eyebrow told me as much.

"I assumed that all of this driving around has made you hungry. You and your friends are not as inconspicuous as you think you are and have a few things to learn when it comes to tailing somebody."

I should have known he would have figured it out. "But... I just have this feeling that there is someone out there planning a murder and I was afraid that, after those letters you had shown me, it would be you."

"Miss Summers," said Detective Shorts, "someone is always planning to commit a crime. That is why we have police. And I am starting to regret showing you that box of letters."

"But—"

"Go home."

Detective Shorts stalked away and got back into his own vehicle, driving off and leaving me in my car, parked on the side of the road holding a hot dog and a soda. My phone rang as Greg called me and I answered it with the hands free calling feature that my car had.

"Mel?" came Greg's voice.

"Yeah."

"We can't find Detective Shorts anywhere. Where are you? What are you doing?"

"Holding a hot dog and a Coke," I replied.

"Huh?"

"He knows we were tailing him," I replied, "and pulled me over to tell us to back off. I'll meet you back at home."

Yep. Plan A did not work out so well. Good thing I had a plan B, because just as Detective Shorts had pulled away, I noticed Jon sitting in the back seat of his car, waving at me.

It didn't take long for me to get back home. Greg and Jackie were already waiting for me. I strolled through the door with the soda Detective Shorts had given me, having already eaten the hot dog. I placed the soda cup on the counter—a wet ring from the condensation on the side formed right away—and set my purse next to it. Frustrated that we were no closer to discovering who those men Jon had overheard were targeting, I said nothing to either Jackie or Greg. What could I say?

"What now?" asked Jackie.

"I wish I knew," I said. I didn't know what to do. I had nothing to go on and unless Jon came up with something while hanging around Detective Shorts, I doubted that we would have anything to go after.

Greg's phone rang. "Jack," he answered.

My ears perked up. Whenever Jack called, he usually delivered some piece of interesting news, or at least had some portion of the current puzzle we worked on.

Greg put the phone on speaker.

"Can you all hear me?" asked Jack.

"Yes," replied Greg.

"I did some digging, but didn't find a whole lot. There are at least three hundred cars whose licenses have the two letters you gave me at the beginning."

My hopes fell. There was no way we would be able to check out 300 different addresses. It would take too long and I had no idea when these men Jon had overheard planned on committing their heinous act.

"Now," continued Jack, "you said that the car was old and rusted, maybe about twenty years, so I was able to eliminate all of those registered within the last fifteen. That knocked the number down to fifty different cars. Do you know the make or model?"

"No," I said. I was never very good at recognizing cars, which company made them, their model, or the year they came off the line. "It was a boxy car."

Both Greg and Jackie looked at me, giving me the "oh that helped a lot" look. I knew it wasn't very helpful, but I had nothing else to give them.

"It could have been a Buick, but I'm not sure," I added.

"Boxy?" said Jack. "It could be an old Buick, but don't quote me on that. I guess you'll just have to check out the fifty addresses."

"Can you…" I began.

"I'm emailing them to you all now," said Jack. "Now, if you all—"

"There is one more thing," I said, getting an idea.

"Of course there is," replied Jack, but I don't think we were supposed to hear him.

"Are there any old file cases of Detective Shorts where the person was convicted and his family might have vowed to get some sort of justice?" I knew what I said didn't make sense, but I was having a little trouble putting my thoughts into words.

"I'm sure that all of the families of the convicted vowed to get some sort of revenge, not wanting to believe that the person they loved could commit such a crime."

Jack's sarcasm came through loud and clear and a part of me wanted to smack him, but I decided to re-phrase my question. "Did any of those he arrested, who were also convicted, die while in prison?"

"That wouldn't be too difficult to find out," said Jack.

We all waited several minutes as he typed on his key-board, listening to the clack-clack of the keys as it came over the phone.

"Anything?" Greg asked when we didn't hear Jack speak for several minutes.

The sounds of more typing answered his question until…

"This is interesting," said Jack. "It's an old case, one from before Detective Shorts became a Detective. He was the arresting officer and provided testimony at the trial. Of course, he wasn't the only one to provide testi-mony. Someone else did as well. But it is believed that his testimony is what sealed the conviction on the defendant. The man died while in prison five years ago."

"What was his name?" I asked.

"Tony Dribbens," said Jack. "He was killed during a prison riot."

"That explains why someone might want revenge," Jackie said.

"This might be why someone would want to harm the detective," commented Greg.

That was what I thought too. "What is the name of the other person who testified?" I asked.

"You'll have to give me a little time on that one," answered Jack. "The records were sealed and it's going to take a little creativity to find out without getting caught."

"All right," I said. "Just let us know when you find out. Thanks." Before Jack hung up, I got an idea. "Did this Tony Dribbens have any relatives?"

I heard Jack typing on the keyboard before he answered. "No. His parents are dead. He had a brother, but his brother died four years ago."

Well, there went that idea. "Well, if you learn anything else, will you let us know."

A long pause followed on the other end and I knew Jack debated telling Greg and me to go jump off a cliff and risk his mother being allowed to come for a visit, or doing what we wanted, knowing Greg would keep his end of the bargain and not invite his mother out at all.

"I'll call you when I know something," said Jack.

"Thanks, buddy," Greg replied.

"Buddy my a—" came Jack's voice as Greg hung up on him.

We looked at each other, each thinking the same thing: that we had nothing to go on. Detective Shorts was still my primary lead for whom the proposed murderers might be after, but even that appeared to be a bit of a stretch without anything more to go on. What were we to do? With nothing else to do, I turned on the TV, hoping that I would be able to relax and perhaps we could brainstorm what to do next.

"And in a breaking story today," said the woman on the television—it turned out that the last channel the TV happened to have been on was the local news—into her microphone, "a local resident was found dead in his home two days ago."

"Didn't they publish that story yesterday?" asked Greg.

"Yeah," replied Jackie, "but sometimes they have to recycle older stories just to have something to talk about."

That was true enough. Sometimes, it seemed as though we got to listen to the same news story 50 times in one day. Jackie reached for the remote to change the channel, but at that moment, an image of the burned house flashed on the screen and I remembered seeing it before in the picture, though what got my attention was an image of a button, matching the one I had found at the amusement park. I stopped her.

"Mr. Farford was known for his drinking and authorities believe that he had passed out with a lit cigarette in his hand, which fell to the carpet, starting the fire."

"What?" asked Jackie.

I took the remote and pressed the rewind button, thankful for the first time that we had DVR. I watched as the images played in reverse until I found what I searched for: the image of the button.

"What's this?" asked Greg.

"Look at it," I said.

Both Jackie and Greg stared at me, not comprehending where I was going. Frustrated, but not surprised because even I almost missed it, I rushed to my room where I had placed the button on my night stand and snatched it, hurrying back out to the living room, holding it out to them. "See? It's the same."

They both looked at the button in my hand and the one pictured on the television screen.

"They look the same," said Greg.

"Exactly," I replied.

"Could they be the same?" asked Jackie. "As in, from the same shirt."

"It's probable," Greg said. "Though, I've never seen one like that before."

"Neither have I," I said, "and it doesn't match any of the buttons on the blouses I have."

"You own blouses?" Jackie blurted out.

I glared at her. We lived in the same apartment, and have shared it for the last two years and she is just now learning that I own a blouse, especially since she was the one who had purchased it for me in the first place. "You know I do. The one that you made me buy last winter."

"Oh, that one. For a moment, I thought you might have actually purchased one yourself."

"The question is," said Greg, "what is this button's twin doing at the burnt remains of an old drunkard's house?"

"Exactly what I was thinking," I said, "and there is only one way to find out."

"I'm not going to get any sleep tonight, am I?" said Jackie.

Chapter 10

We parked down the street out of sight of Henry Farford's home, waiting for the last of the stragglers who had stopped to observe the reporter give her news story on the air to leave, thankful for the fact that the sun had gone down and we had darkness on our side. Once clear, we hurried over to the house, sneaking across the lawn, being careful not to trip over the broken lawn chairs that littered it. The door hung on its hinges and Greg held it open for Jackie and me as we slipped inside the skeletal remains of the house.

"Are you sure we'll find this button?" asked Greg as he stepped on a splintered and charred piece of wood that had fallen from the ceiling.

I just shrugged. I had no idea if we would find it or

not, but wanted to try. Besides, it didn't make sense that it would be there in a house that had caught fire by accident, unless it was no accident. But then, how did the two know each other?

We meandered through soot and ash, the dark silt covering our clothes and skin within moments of us entering the burned home. I picked through the torn and blackened adult magazines that littered what was left of the floor. Not much guesswork involved in what Mr. Farford liked to do in his spare time.

"Well that figures," said Jackie and I hushed her for being too loud. "Sorry," she whispered.

I didn't want anyone overhearing us, or Detective Shorts discovering where we were. Jackie pointed out a cabinet—the lock had been broken—with half-empty, or very nearly empty, bottles of vodka, Jack Daniels, tequila, rum, and whiskey. A dusting of soot covered them, but the bottles seemed to have been intact, despite the flames that had ravaged the rest of the residence.

Jackie snatched one of the bottles and sloshed the liquid around inside of it. "Everything else is burned, except for the alcohol."

I shared her sentiment and smiled as she plopped the bottle back on the shelf, thinking of how ironic it was that the very thing that put the man into a state where he had started a fire without knowing it, survived the blaze.

"Hey guys," Greg called us. "Over here!"

Jackie and I crowded around him, wondering what he had found. I did not understand what he tried to show us and Greg must have guessed that I was a bit confused. He brought up the flashlight app on his phone and shined the blue LED light on it. The black spot was darker than the rest of the marks around it, but I still did not see what he was getting at.

"Look at how this is a nice circle and then the black mark kind of fans out, kind of like how a fire spreads," said Greg. "This must be the origin of the fire itself."

"Well, yeah," replied Jackie. "It was started by a lit cigarette that he dropped. This must be where it hit the floor."

"But look where the chair is," Greg said.

I looked at what was left of the chair, which resembled a small pile of ashes more than an easy chair. The black mark appeared to be a little too far away from the chair. "He must have long arms," I commented.

"Think about it"—Greg snatched another chair in the house that had escaped being destroyed and placed it where the easy chair had been—"if he was sitting here, passed out, he'd be leaning somewhat like this." He mimicked how a person might be positioned if they had fallen asleep in the chair. "And his arms should be hanging more straight downward, not at an angle."

"But that would put the fallen cigarette in this area," said Jackie.

"Exactly," Greg replied. "In order for the lit stub to fall here, the guy would have to have been positioned like this in his chair and his arm out more horizontally, but that's a little hard to do in a chair." Greg mimed what he meant so that we could picture it.

"So, you're saying that it was arson," said Jackie.

"It could have been," said Greg. "Just think, the

positioning is a little off when you compare where the fire must have started and where the man was seated."

I pressed my hand against the charred remains of the carpet, wishing I could wash them right away as the grime covered them, and sniffed. Alcohol. The whole carpet seemed to have been soaked in it. "There's alcohol all over the floor."

"Of course there is," said Jackie. "An alcoholic lived here."

I gave her a look.

"Well, he was one," Jackie replied, "and have you ever known an alcoholic to be a good housekeeper?"

I glanced around at the empty bottles, open magazines strewn all over the place, and burnt food wrappers. I cringed to think what might be living in the carpet, considering the guy probably never vacuumed. "No, I can't say that I have. Perfect cover, though."

"I'll say," said Greg. "With all of the liquor bottles around, you have the makings of a bomb. One spark and this place would just go up. Wouldn't take long."

"Then why kill him?" asked Jackie. "The guy was a known alcoholic. He's been seen at every bar in town and was well-known for buying his favorite drink by the liter, along with his favorite pack of smokes. Murdering him makes no sense."

"Unless he saw something he shouldn't have," I muttered. "We need to find that button, if it's here."

Jackie cocked her head at me and I knew what she thought: how were we supposed to do that? The place was a mess and I had no idea where to start looking. I thought back to the video and pulled out my phone, pulling up the web browser app. One thing about this modern age, just about anything that was aired on television made it to the internet within hours where you could download it. I went to the news station's website and found the video they had aired earlier. Relieved that I had found it, I pressed play and watched the video, waiting for them to do their tour of the house. Once the image with the button showed up, I paused the video.

The different lighting made it more of a challenge for me to figure out where in the house that button was when the camera rolled over it, but I tried to picture the house as it would have appeared in the daylight. I meandered around the area with my phone in one hand, while I searched for the spot on the video. Jackie and Greg both watched while I wandered to the kitchen, stepping over a pipe and what was left of the stove, heading for what should have been the back door, but all that remained now was a hole in the wall. I checked the video again and bent low to the floor, using the light emitted by my phone's screen to see what I was doing.

"Mel?" said Jackie.

I dropped to my knees, running my hand over the layer of ash that covered the kitchen floor, while looking at the image on my phone. If I had guessed right, this should be the same area as what was depicted on the video. I continued to run my hand over the floor, growing more frustrated as I turned up nothing, until my hand brushed something unusual. I flipped on the flashlight app of my own phone and focused it where my hand was, digging through the soot, bringing up a small round button that glittered a little in the light. I held it up for Greg and Jackie to see.

Greg took it and studied it. "This definitely looks unique."

"Too unique," I said, "for someone like Mr. Farford to have. And"—I pulled the button I had found at the amusement park out of my pocket, holding it next to the one I had just discovered—"they are the same."

Greg took them, studying them. "They do look similar."

"And they look just like the buttons I saw on the sleeve of that guy's shirt when I was at the convenience store."

"But you didn't see his face," said Jackie.

My heart sank at that. I wish I had gotten a good look at his face.

"I'm sorry," said Jackie, realizing she had struck a nerve, "I didn't mean to..."

"No, it's okay," I said. "You're right. I didn't get a look at his face."

"We need to get these buttons looked at," said Greg. "They are too unique to have been manufactured. Does Tiny know anyone who might be able to help us?"

"He might," I replied.

A car drove past the house, causing us to jump a little and I realized how late it was. We had gotten what we had come for, so I suggested that we should leave, to which both Greg and Jackie agreed. None of us wanted to get caught for trespassing, nor did we want to get in trouble for inadvertently impeding an arson investigation. I made a mental note to call Jack, hoping that he would be able to tell us what the official ruling was on that, since the news had made no mention of it.

We hurried down the street to Greg's car and went home, where I fell into bed still wearing my soot-covered clothes.

Chapter 11

My eyes refused to open as my foggy mind struggled to wake up, realizing that it was morning and hours had passed since I had fallen asleep. I rubbed the sand from my eyes, which still hurt as I opened them and they focused in the bright sunlight that filled my room. I glanced at my watch, which lay on my nightstand, and bolted upright. I had to be at work in half an hour! I never heard my alarm go off. I snatched my phone and checked its clock, hoping that my watch was wrong and that I really had more time. Nope. It was correct, and now I have 28 minutes.

"Jackie!" I screamed, jumping out of bed and ripping my clothes off from the day before. "Jackie, we're late!"

Her door creaked open and she shuffled out into the hallway, yawning and scratching her side. "What's wrong?"

"We're late," I told her, poking my head out my bedroom door.

"We can't be that late," she said through half a yawn. "Why it's only"—she glanced at the digital clock in her room—"Oh, crap!" I chuckled as Jackie rushed back into her room, slamming the door shut.

I hurried into the bathroom, grabbing the can of dry shampoo I had and sprayed it on my hair, while trying to also put on some makeup, with disastrous results. While Jackie rummaged around in her room, I ran back to my own, grabbing the first thing from my dresser that I knew had been washed, and threw on some shoes, before racing into the kitchen to pack a lunch for us and for Greg, as I had promised to make him something to take to work. Too bad that his homemade lunch would consist of PB&J and a bag of chips, which reminded me that I needed to go grocery shopping.

"I'm ready," said Jackie, snatching her purse from the table by the door. "You're not going to work in that, are you?"

I gave her an odd glance, wondering how in 5 minutes she managed to look as though she was going to a fashion show. Jackie nodded her head in my direction and I moved over to the floor length mirror we had in the hallway and made a mental note to clean out my dresser. In my haste, I managed to grab the same pair of jeans and a t-shirt (which said "Kiss me baby!") that I had worn since high school and cringed. I didn't have time to change, but started for my room anyway, only to be stopped by Jackie, snatching my arm, throwing a semi-sheer shawl over my shoulders, and pushing me out the door, with me somehow managing to snatch the brown paper bags with our lunches in them.

Opening the door, Jackie and I both rushed out, running right into Greg.

"Morning, sunshine," he greeted me.

I gave him a quick kiss, shoved a lunch bag into his hands, and ran off.

"What's the hurry?" he asked.

"We have"—I glanced at my watch—"eighteen minutes to get to work."

"What?" Gregg looked at his watch. "Oh, peanuts! I overslept too!"

"And you're just now figuring this out," said Jackie.

"You two go," he said. "I'll see you all later."

I gave Greg another kiss as I ran off with Jackie.

"What? You didn't cut the crust off?" he joked, winking at me.

Jackie and I made it to the garage, where we piled into her car, and sped off for downtown. Traffic was heavy (typical when you're running late), but at least she knew of a few backroads she could take to avoid most of it. We parked as close to the Candle Shoppe as we could and ran for the door, managing to squeak in about a minute after the hour. Before I clocked in, I skidded to a halt and Jackie bumped into me.

"Hey," she said, but stopped when she noticed Tammy, and her hat: a bright, neon green with a miniature grasshopper and crickets glued along the sides.

"Hi, guys!" she greeted in a cheery voice.

Jackie peeked around me, took one look at the hat, and whispered, "I don't want to know."

She and I proceeded to the back where we signed in

and put our stuff in our lockers, before hurrying back out to the main room to avoid being yelled at for being late. I did not get to avoid such admonition.

"Running a little late, aren't you?" said Jon, but only I heard or saw him.

"Late night," I whispered back.

Jon glanced at Tammy and her grasshopper hat. "I'm serious," he said in a flat tone, "just let me get the bug spray and—"

"No!" I hissed at him.

"All right, fine," Jon agreed, "but she's scaring me, so you can imagine what she's doing to the customers."

So, Tammy's antics are enough to scare a ghost. I'll try to remember that in the future.

The store remained empty of customers and I remembered the buttons, wondering whom I should contact to learn their significance. Only one name came to mind: Tiny. I pulled out my phone and texted him.

Buttons? came his reply.

Do you know someone or not?

Yeah, I know a guy. Will bring him by.

Tiny's last message ended that conversation and I put my phone back in my pocket. I had no idea when Tiny planned to show up with this guy he knew. He didn't always tell you when he planned to stop by. I just hoped it would happen soon. As it turned out, I did not have to wait long. About two hours after I had contacted Tiny, he showed up at the Candle Shoppe with a man who looked as though he was none too happy to find himself dragged to some candle store.

"I brought what you asked for," said Tiny as he stepped through the door.

Jackie and I shared a look, before glancing in Tammy's direction, but she was busy rearranging the tea light candles into a house of cards, so to speak, because whatever she tried to build kept falling over. I motioned for Tiny to follow me to a more secluded area of the store, near the back, but far enough away from Mr. Stilton's office that he would not see us if he chose to come out.

"When I said that I would help," said the man Tiny had brought with him, "I didn't mean that as permission for you to drag me over here."

Tiny glared at him and shoved him closer to me.

The man changed his mind about protesting. "He says you found some interesting buttons."

I pulled the two buttons I had found (one from the amusement park and the other from the burned remains of the house) and held them out to him.

The man reached for them, wearing a style of shirt I had only seen in the movies, making me wonder if he had been performing in a play.

"Are you part of a theater troupe?" I asked, trying to break the uncomfortable silence that followed as he studied the buttons.

"No," replied the man, holding a magnifying glass to his eye, while bending low over the buttons in his palm. "This is my normal clothing."

"Zeke, here," said Tiny, "sort of lives in the past. He likes old stuff and handmade stuff and likes to dress as though he's from the 1600s."

"1718 to be exact," said the man Tiny identified as Zeke. "This stitching gives it away that this shirt is a representation of the style worn back in 1718."

"And only you would know that," muttered Tiny.

"The buttons?" I asked, wanting to avoid being caught in the middle of their disagreement. The displeasure in being dragged from his home still filled Zeke's voice.

"They're nothing special," said Zeke. When he noticed the disgruntled expression on our faces, he continued. "I don't mean that they are not significant, but they are not historic either. Look, see these uneven notches here?"

Zeke held the buttons out to me and gave me the magnifying glass, allowing me to study them and I saw the notches he referred to.

"Notice how they are uneven?"

I nodded.

"That is a sign of having been made by hand. These markings here also mean that a machine never touched these buttons. Modern buttons are smooth, even, and uniform—that is how you can tell that they are made by machines. But these are a bit misshapen, which only a magnifying glass will reveal, and the grooves here are all unique. No matter how hard a person tries, they can never achieve the uniformity of a machine. That being said, these buttons don't seem to be very old. Maybe… only twenty years, so they have no historical value. Not yet, anyway."

"Why would someone wear handmade buttons?" I asked.

"Why would anyone make them?" said Tiny, thinking that making such a thing was a waste of time.

"Several reasons," said Zeke. "Some people find that

constructing something with their hands is relaxing and a good stress reliever." He gave Tiny a pointed look. "The only reason I can think of for why a person would wear these is if he made them himself, likes unique things, or they were made by someone important to him and given to him as a gift."

"So why does he keep losing them?" I wondered out loud and Zeke heard me.

"It could be that the person who wears these needs to learn how to sew them on the shirt better." He handed me the buttons and looked at Tiny. "May I go now?"

Tiny's expression darkened a little bit at being talked to in such a way, but he huffed out a lungful of air, saying, "Fine."

"How do you two know each other?" I asked.

"He wanted a unique tattoo," said Zeke, "and that just happened to be the day I accidentally stumbled into a tattoo parlor, looking for a phone I could use because my car broke down. I noticed the… artwork and commented on how it was an inaccurate representation of a hat typically worn by Henry VIII. A slight argument ensued and before I knew it, I found myself in the chair getting a tattoo."

"May I see it?" I said, my curiosity getting the better of me, and Zeke did not strike me as the sort of man who would get a tattoo.

The man lifted his shirt. "It's the North Star, something that any sailor, before modern radar and navigational systems, would use to guide their ship through the high seas."

"Cool," I said.

Zeke put his shirt back down, bid Tiny and me farewell, and left.

Though Zeke cleared up the mystery of the button, as far as how they might have been made, I was still no closer to knowing who they belonged to.

Jackie tapped me on the shoulder. "So?" she whispered to me.

"They're handmade, like we thought, but no idea who owned them," I replied.

Jackie noticed the disappointment in my voice and patted my back in a comforting motion. "You'll figure it out. You always do."

I smiled at her and walked over to a set of shelves where the candles had gotten out of order from customers picking them up and putting them down wherever they pleased. As I rearranged them, putting the obvious nicked ones in the back, I had a thought. The man whom Detective Shorts arrested all that time ago, his trial would have been in the papers, and most news articles are on the internet now. Maybe I could try and look it up. I slipped away from the well-lit aisle I was in to a corner that was more out of the way and in shadow, making it more difficult for Mr. Stilton to see me while I pulled out my phone and brought up a web browser. I did a quick search for "man arrested" and then typed in the year Jack had given me earlier. A bunch of results came up about people arrested for murder within the last two years, but none of that was what I looked for. Annoyed, I typed in another search term, making certain to put it in quotation marks. I tapped the first result. Nope. Nothing. Just an editorial piece about how too many people are being convicted of murder these days. Could it be because they are committing more crimes? Pushing my personal thoughts aside, I tapped on the one below it. The name Tony Dribbens appeared in the article and my heart skipped a beat as I remembered that being the name Jack had given me of a man convicted of murder and dying in prison.

Family Mourns Trial Outcome

The jury gave their verdict today in a trial that has rocked the county. Tony Dribbens has been found guilty of first degree manslaughter and has been sentenced to 20 years in a maximum security prison with no chance for parole.

"I can't believe it," the mother cried when asked for an interview.

"The Dribbens family is saddened by this verdict and will appeal this decision," said the family's attorney. "Justice has not been served today."

The detective on the case declined to be interviewed, instead directing all questions towards the prosecuting attorney.

"We cannot be more pleased with the outcome," said the prosecuting attorney. "A dangerous man has been taken off the streets and the victim's family can now find peace."

I skimmed over the rest of the article, scrolling to the bottom where a few images were. Several of them were of the trial and the people standing outside the courtroom afterward. One panged my heart: an image of Mrs. Dribbens in tears over losing her son, while another showed the mother of the victim crying just as much—I guess these sorts of things hurt both sides—but one image did not seem to belong. It looked a bit faded, as though it had been printed, locked away someplace, before being dug out and scanned into the computer. The image showed two boys with their arms around each other's shoulders, smiling for the camera and a caption underneath it that read, "Tony as a child."

Tony wore a t-shirt while the boy next to him had a button up shirt on. I double tapped the image, blowing it up and zoomed in. I enlarged it as best I could, the grainy image making it a little difficult to get a clear picture, but I managed to get it focused enough for me to make out what I wanted to see: the sleeve buttons. I held one of the buttons I had found, which I kept with me at all times for now, and compared it to the one in the image. They matched.

So the mysterious man with the buttons knew this Tony Dribbens. *What was the relationship?* I wondered, not that it all that important since the most significant thing was that he seemed to be the focal point in this plot to murder someone, but I still didn't know who the intended victim was. If only I knew where to find him now. Frustrated that I didn't know what to do next, I decided to just keep myself busy at work, while I waited for my lunch break, though I had a feeling that I wouldn't be allowed to go anyplace since I was still on probation for being late earlier this week.

When noon rolled around, I clocked out for lunch. Tammy and Jackie both told me to hurry back so that they could take their break, since we were no longer allowed to take our breaks at the same time. "I will," I told them, "but I need to get something from across the street."

Jackie gave me a doubtful look as though she read my thoughts, but this time I had no ulterior motive. I had forgotten to bring something to eat, only because when I thought I had placed my bagged lunch in the car, I had really dropped it on the floor of the parking garage, which meant I had to go to the café across the street to get something.

"I'll be quick," I promised, grabbing my purse and hurrying out the door to the small restaurant right across from us. It was more of a deli / coffee shop where you could get a sandwich, or burger if you really wanted one, ice cold drinks, and coffee. I had been there several times in the past two years and their food was decent. What I liked about it was that it wasn't a chain restaurant, but locally owned.

"May I help you," greeted the cashier as I entered the café.

"Yes," I said, already knowing what I wanted as I tended to get the same thing each time. "I'll have your ham and cheese on rye with the Dijon mustard and chipotle sauce."

"With lettuce, tomatoes, avocado, and pickles?"

"Yes." The lady knew me too well. She almost always took my order and knew what I wanted. On some days, she had my sandwich made minutes before I arrived, one of the perks of being predictable I guess. "And a—"

"Pineapple-Strawberry smoothie," said the woman.

I smiled at her and nodded my head.

"That will be eleven dollars and sixty-six cents," said the woman and I handed her $15 in cash.

Within minutes, my order was ready and I took the paper bag, thanking the cashier, and left, sipping my smoothie as I walked out the door. It was my favorite flavor and I always seemed to down it before I finished my sandwich. As I waited for a break in the traffic so that I could cross the street, I spotted a man putting up flyers for the upcoming talent show that would be hosted at the amusement park. Curious, I moseyed over to read one of them, ignoring the man at first. While I glanced at the flyer, I pulled out my phone to check the time, not wanting to be late again, and while doing so, one of the buttons fell out and dropped on the pavement. The man picked it up for me, rotating it in his fingers, interested in it.

"Interesting button you have there," he commented, placing it in my outstretched hand.

"Um... family heirloom," I said, putting it back in my pocket and turning to go.

"Can't be too valuable."

I stopped, my curiosity piqued. "Why do you say that?"

"I know a guy who wears a shirt that has that same button."

"Oh?" I said.

"Yeah, he works where I do."

"Where do you work?" I tried to make my question sound innocent, despite the fact that the flyers the man put up and his shirt gave away his place of employment.

"The new amusement park," replied the man, and

judging by the light tone in his voice, he didn't seem offended at all. "You been there, yet?"

"Yes, I went with a couple of friends. We didn't get to try everything, but we had fun."

"You should come back. Some new rides just opened."

"I'll do that," I said, glancing at the time on my phone and realizing I needed to get back to the Candle Shoppe ASAP, before Mr. Stilton started to wonder where I was and fire me for being derelict in my duties.

I glanced both ways down the street and dashed across in between cars, bursting through the door just as my boss stepped out of his office.

"You're late," he snapped.

I held up my sandwich bag, saying, "There was a bit of a line at the café across the street. I wasn't the only one who decided to eat there."

"Liar," said Jon, but only I heard him.

Mr. Stilton seemed to have bought my story and turned away. "Jackie, you can go take your lunch now, but hurry back in case Tammy needs to buy a lunch."

"Oh, I brought mine," said Tammy, jumping up and down, waving a plastic lunchbox. She opened it up and pulled out a sandwich—at least, I think that's what it was—stuffed with green, mushy slop that smelled worse than a rotten egg.

"What is that?" asked Jackie with a disgusted look on her face.

"Avocado surprise," replied Tammy. "It's mashed avocado with mayonnaise mixed in and some red pepper and salt, tuna, and crackers."

"Sounds revolting," Jon murmured to me.

Tammy took a bite of her sandwich, covered her mouth, and ran to the bathroom, followed by retching sounds.

Jackie shook her head. "I told her to put it in the fridge," she said to me as she walked by.

"Jackie!" I pulled her aside when Mr. Stilton disappeared in the back room again.

"Mel, I want to get something to eat."

"I think I know where we should look next," I told her, glancing at Jon and hoping he would listen in. "To find the person behind the murder plot," I added when she gave me a confused look.

"Where?"

"The amusement park itself."

Jackie gave me a doubtful look.

"While I was out getting my lunch—"

"Which is what I would like to do."

"While I was out, I ran into someone who works at the park and was putting flyers up. He recognized the buttons we found. Said they belonged to someone who works at the park."

"That is sort of what we thought anyway."

"Yeah, but this confirms it," I said.

"We need to have another look around that place," said Jon to me.

"That's what I want to do," I replied.

"You know," said Jackie, "it is very rude to be talking amongst yourselves while I am here."

Jon materialized, since Mr. Stilton had gone back to his office and Tammy was still in the bathroom.

"Perhaps you should be more intuitive like your ancestors," mocked Jon.

"Shouldn't you be in school?" replied Jackie.

"Enough, you two," I hissed at them. "Greg gets off about the same time we do. We should meet him there."

Jackie nodded in agreement.

"And you"—I turned to Jon—"can help us blend in as employees."

"Fine," agreed Jon. "But you better be there by six sharp and not a minute late."

"Hey guys?"

Tammy approached us looking so ashen, that even the embroidered fireflies on her skirt looked miserable. "I don't feel so great. I think an avocado surprise sandwich sounded more appetizing that it was."

"It doesn't sound appetizing at all," Jon muttered to me, having turned invisible again.

"And I didn't even add the mayonnaise to it until this morning," moaned Tammy, holding her stomach.

"You mean, when you got to work?" asked Jackie.

Tammy nodded.

"You used the mayonnaise in the refrigerator in the back room?" Jackie asked, incredulous.

Tammy nodded again.

"That's been in there for over two years! It's a science experiment, like everything else in that fridge."

"And none of you thought to throw it away when it expired two years ago?" Jon whispered to me. His sarcasm did not go unnoticed.

"We're all just a little afraid of what might be lurking in there," I said out of the side of my mouth, hoping that Tammy was too sick to notice.

"Apparently," replied Jon, "since the mayonnaise seems to be a real killer."

Tammy looked so horrible, that I felt bad for her. "You should go home. I'll tell Mr. Stilton that you aren't feeling well."

Tammy shuffled to where her purse was stuffed under the counter and pulled out her keys, hanging her head low and looking like she might throw up again at any moment.

"I'll drive you," said Jackie, snatching her keys. "And I'm taking this." She grabbed the paper bag with my sandwich in it.

"Would you like my smoothie as well?" I asked her.

"You finished it already!"

After Tammy headed for the door, Jon reminded us to not be late. "I mean it. Six sharp."

He vanished.

"He's a little moody, you know that?" Jackie said to me as she left with Tammy wobbling in front of her.

I texted Greg about our plans and he replied with an enthusiastic "I'll be there" before heading to Mr. Stilton's office to inform him about Tammy's mishap.

Chapter 12

Jackie and I walked up to the front gate of the small amusement park where Greg waited for us, glad to be out of the Candle Shoppe, and Mr. Stilton's watchful gaze, which had been a recent development. People shuffled in and out of the gates, some with their arms full of prizes they had won from the various games, or items they had purchased from the gift store. Many of the parents looked exhausted while their children still had the same energy leaving that they had going in.

"Hey," I greeted Greg, giving him a hug.

"So, what's the plan?" he asked.

"Get inside and find Jon," I said.

We walked up to the gate and scanned our passes. Once inside, I looked around for Jon, wondering how I would spot a ghost in this sea of people as they wandered about in a haphazard manner with no discernable pattern.

"PSSST!"

I turned to my left and saw Jon standing behind a hot dog stand, waving me over. "This way," I said to Jackie and Greg.

When we headed for him, Jon turned and moved away from us, but made sure not to go too far, or too fast, so that way we would not lose him. I kept close watch of where he went, following his every move, making certain that Jackie and Greg stayed close behind. No one paid much attention to us—too wrapped up in their own world—except for those I had bumped into by accident in my efforts to keep up. Jon led us to a building near the edge of the compound where few tourists were and ducked around a corner. I chased after him.

"Jon?" I called when I didn't see him, turning in circles, hoping to spot him, while Jackie and Greg hopped from one foot to the other as they waited for the next set of instructions. "Jon?"

"Over here!"

Jon's voice came from my right and a blue, steel door swung open, waiting for me to catch it. I took hold of it and waved Jackie and Greg inside.

"Come on!" said Jon from the bottom of the steps.

We hurried down the metal stairs as the door shut behind us, our movements causing them to rattle a bit, despite our attempts at being silent. We entered a dim hallway that echoed with the hollow sounds of others moving around in the building; I just hoped that they remained unaware of our presence.

"Jon?" I whispered.

"Here," he whispered back.

When I turned towards him, I realized that he stood in a locker room. "What's this?" I asked.

"You need uniforms," replied Jon. "This is the best place to get them. Now hurry! You never know when someone might walk in."

We each ran to a locker, pulling on the doors, looking for any that had been left open. Greg found one first. He pulled out a shirt and tossed it to Jackie, "This looks like it might fit you best."

Jackie caught it and glared at it a moment before slipping it on over her sleeveless, ruffle blouse. "It doesn't match my pants."

"Or your shoes," mumbled Jon, rolling his eyes.

I tugged on locker door after locker door, but none of them were unlocked and passed an abandoned toolbox as I searched. Frustrated, and growing tired of searching, I hurried to the toolbox and flung it open, finding a screwdriver, which I snatched. Using the screwdriver, I rammed it into the side of a locker door and jimmied it open. but not without causing a small dent and some scratches. Both Greg and Jackie watched with amusement.

"You've been spending too much time with Tiny," joked Jackie.

"Perhaps," I replied, "but he does know some useful skills."

Two shirts and a pair of crumpled up pants lay on the bottom of the locker. I seized the shirts and handed one to Greg.

"You know," said Greg, reading the nametag on the shirt, "I don't think I look like an Izzy."

I smiled at him and cringed when I saw the nametag on my shirt: Luigi. Really?

Jackie covered her mouth to suppress a laugh, but a few snorts escaped her fingers anyway. "Now all we need is a nametag that says, 'Mario' and we'll be all set."

"That can be arranged," I told her.

Footsteps stopped in the doorway of the locker room and I knew we had been caught. "What are you all doing in here?" demanded the man who had walked in on us.

Before any of us had a chance to answer, Jon materialized, saying, "Will you all hurry up? We don't have…"

The man gawked at Jon with a horrified expression on his face.

"What are you staring at?" Jon demanded, as though seeing a ghost for the first time should be a natural thing.

The man fainted, crashing onto the floor with a thud.

"What do we do with him?" asked Jackie.

Jon shrugged his shoulders. "Just stuff him in a locker." He disappeared again.

I helped Greg pick the man up and seat him on one of the benches in the room while Jackie grabbed an abandoned towel on the floor and tucked it around the poor guy like you would a blanket.

"What?" she said when she caught me giving her a look. "Now it looks like he just decided to take a nap."

We hurried out of the locker room and back outside, grabbing three cleaning carts along the way, without being noticed, for which I was thankful because I had no idea how I would explain all of this to Detective Shorts if we had gotten caught.

"Now what?" asked Jackie when went outside.

"Let's set the timers on our phones for an hour. We'll split up. If you find anyone suspicious, try to eavesdrop on them. But when the hour is up, we come back here."

"Deal," said Jackie.

"You be careful," Greg told me, pulling me aside.

"I will."

I watched him walk off—Jackie had already disappeared—before I sped away with my cart, heading straight for the plaza where the big grandfather clock was.

People bumped into me, knocking my cart around, as I attempted to navigate through the meandering crowd of park-goers, who paid little attention to where they were going as they were more interested in looking at all of the rides. I managed to get through, though I did have to sweep up a few spills. One woman had dropped her popcorn and when she saw me, she dragged me over to where the mess was, demanding to know why I hadn't cleaned it up yet and threatening to tell my supervisor.

"Go right ahead," I had told her, handing her the broom and dustpan. "Why don't you sweep it up yourself, instead of expecting someone else to clean up your mess?"

"Why I never!" She threw the broom down in disgust as a few in the crowd watched us.

"Oh, go tell someone who cares," I retorted.

I grabbed my cart and hurried away, pushing it down the walk at such a fast pace that the wheels threatened to come off. When I reached the plaza, I slowed down and headed for the overflowing trash can. I watched the people who passed by, while pulling the garbage out of the can, placing it in my cart, and sticking a new bag in the can itself. I had to keep up my charade. I noticed two men locked in the middle of an argument; their animated arm movements made it clear that they had been going at it for a while. Remembering that Jon had mentioned that it was two men he had overheard the night he died, I maneuvered my cart near where they were.

A cup plopped on the concrete next to my feet, spilling the soda that it had contained and splashing my tennis shoes. Annoyed, but knowing I had to maintain my ruse, I pulled out a gray rag, that smelled like it had been soaked in water from a clogged sink that had mosquito larvae living in it, and wiped up the mess. When I was almost finished, a man strolled passed and dropped his half-eaten corn dog on me. I picked it up and prepared to throw it at him, but changed my mind, deciding that he was not worth it.

I looked in the direction of the two men who were still locked in their argument. Taking a broom and dustpan, I crept closer, pretending to sweep as I went.

"I told you not to do it," one of the men said.

"You're not the boss of me," spat the other.

"Quite acting like you are five. You screwed up and you know it."

"Yeah, because you are so much better than me."

"Hey, I'm not the one who cheated on my girlfriend."

"I didn't—do you mind?"

I stopped what I was doing. Both men glared at me, displeased about my listening in. "Sorry," I said, "just trying to do my job."

"Does that include you eavesdropping on other people's private conversations?" one of them demanded.

"Well if you weren't standing where I needed to sweep, then I wouldn't be standing so close where I can't help but overhear that you cheated on your girlfriend," I shouted back.

The moment I had said it, I wanted to bite my tongue and take it back. What was with me? I think all the time I had spent with Rachel had made me more confrontational.

They left.

Releasing a huge sigh, I walked back to the cart and put the broom and the dustpan back on the tray just as the timer on my phone went off. That hour went by fast. I was just about to head back to where Jackie, Greg, and I had agreed to meet when I spotted Jon standing by the grandfather clock, looking sorrowful. He didn't even notice, or seem to care about the two kids that had opened the door to the inner workings of the clock, running away when their mother called them over and leaving it hanging open. Feeling bad for him, and realizing that I had never offered my condolences for his accidental and unexpected demise, I moseyed over to him to speak with him.

"That's one of them," he whispered to me when I reached him.

"What?" It took me a moment to realize what he had meant.

"That man." He pointed at two men, one dressed as a janitor, talking in hushed tones. "I recognize his voice."

I hid behind the clock, trying to listen in.

"I'm sorry, sir," said the one dressed as a janitor, pretending to be apologetic about something.

"Sorry?" replied the other.

The janitor said nothing.

"You ruined my good shirt!" The man stormed away while the janitor muttered something under his breath.

"Are you sure he is one of them?" I asked Jon, who nodded in response.

I turned back around, but the janitor had gone. Hoping to follow him, I scooted around the clock, trying to not look suspicious, but found no sign of the man. I headed back to the front of the clock where Jon was when strong hands seized me from behind and shoved me inside the clock, locking the door behind me.

"Hey!" I screamed, banging on the door.

"Ladies and gentlemen," said a voice over the loudspeakers, "the park is about to close. Please make your way to the nearest exit."

"Hey!" I slammed my fists against the door, pounding it as hard as I could, but it was of no use. No one heard me. "Let me out!"

"Mel?"

"Jon!"

"Mel, can you get out?"

"The door is locked," I replied. "I need you to open it."

"I'm not sure how."

My heart fell. Jon had only been a ghost for a few days and hadn't had time to learn how to move things at will, unlike Rachel who could from the day I had first met her, but she had already been a spirit for over a year by then. "Get Greg and Jackie!"

"There should be a long poker looking thing in there," said Jon.

I reached for my phone so that I could text Greg and use the flashlight app on it. It was not in my pocket. It must have fallen out.

"Have you found it?"

"I can't see anything."

"Reach towards the bottom," he said.

I tried to find the bottom of the clock, but was too big to maneuver. My fingers brushed something and I yanked it free, creating a creaking sound, which rattled my ears. "I found something."

"See if you can use it to poke a hole though the side. The clock may be made from solid wood, but I noticed that there was some rot on the sides when I was fixing it."

I tried ramming the rod against the side of the clock, but despite my best efforts, I could not get the leverage I needed. "I can't!"

Claustrophobia started to set in as the air weighed down my shoulders and felt heavier with every breath I took.

"I'll get help," said Jon. "Just breathe slow and steady."

He was gone.

I beat my fists against the sides of the clock again, screaming at the top of my lungs, hoping someone would hear me, but no one ever came. Sweat dripped down my face as I struggle to open the door, ramming my shoulder into it, but the cramped space prevented me from getting the momentum I needed.

"Help!" I cried again, but knew it would be useless as the noise outside faded.

My breathing quickened and panic set in. Where was Jon? What was taking him so long to get help? Who had shoved me in here? And why?

I heard footsteps outside.

"Hello? Anyone there?"

"Mel!"

"Greg! The door is stuck!"

I had no idea how long I had been inside the clock, but my head spun and I felt light-headed.

Pounding and rustling sounded on the other side as Greg wrestled with the door in an effort to open it. I pushed against it at the same time, putting all of my weight into it until it burst open and I sprang out of there into Greg's arms, sucking in as much air as my lungs would hold.

"Didn't I tell you to be careful?" he said to me, holding me close.

"Mel!" Jackie slammed into me, almost knocking me and Greg over. "When you didn't show up, we knew something had happened."

"How did you get locked in there anyway?" asked Greg.

"I noticed Jon standing here and I decided to talk with him when someone shoved me inside and locked the door."

"Do you know who it is?" asked Greg.

"I didn't see his face," I replied, "and I dropped my phone." I scanned the area for it, but did not find it. Could the person who had pushed me inside the clock have taken it?

Greg called my phone, but we never heard it ring, which meant that it was nowhere in the area. "We should go," he said.

I agreed. We took our borrowed uniforms and carts back to the building that had the locker room in it and left them by the door, before sneaking out the front gate, pretending to be a few stragglers who had not wanted to leave.

When we got back to the apartment, I flopped in the big chair, exhausted and not sure what to do next. Where was my phone? A thought struck me.

"Guys," I said, "do you think that the person who had shoved me in the clock could have my phone?"

"I'd say that it is a distinct possibility," said Jon, making himself heard to everyone, but remained unseen.

"Well, that's not good," Jackie chimed in.

Not good that I lost my phone, but what if…

"That might not be true," I said.

"Huh?" Jackie looked at me with a confused look and I remembered the one time she had lost her phone; she had gone ballistic trying to find it because she didn't want to have to get a new one and try to redownload music, contacts, and anything else she had saved on it.

"We can use it against him," I replied, "assuming that he still has it."

"You're assuming that he took it in the first place," Greg said.

"Yes, I am." I looked at them, incensed that they were not on board with the idea brewing in my mind. "What's wrong?"

"You got locked inside a clock," answered Greg.

Okay. I saw his point. "But if we don't do something, a man might die."

"We should go to Detective Shorts," suggested Jackie.

"With what?" I asked her. "We have no proof of any murder being planned, no idea who shoved me in the clock, and no idea who the intended victim is, other than a hunch that it's Detective Shorts himself."

"Yeah, that does put a damper in things."

"What are you thinking of doing?" Greg asked me with his arms crossed, knowing me too well.

"Setting a trap."

"On one condition," Greg replied, "we bring Tiny."

"Whatever it is, I'm down with it."

We all jumped, turning around and finding Tiny standing in the open doorway. Didn't I lock that?

"How did you…" I began.

"Uh… it was unlocked."

I watched as Tiny shoved the tool he used for picking locks into his pocket, and knew just how he had gotten inside, which was how he entered most residences when he didn't knock.

"What are you doing here?" asked Jackie.

"I tried texting Mel, but she never replied so I thought I'd stop by and see if everything is okay, considering…"

Yep. Tiny knew me too well also.

"So, what's this idea of yours?" he asked.

"Catching a potential murderer," said Jon, remaining invisible and garnering an odd glance from Tiny. Though he had become accustomed to the fact that ghosts sometimes show up when I'm around, it never made it any easier to deal with one that spoke so he could hear it.

"I believe that one of the people Jon had overhead has my phone and—"

"How did he get your phone?" Tiny crossed his arms.

"—I want to see if I can—"

"How did he get your phone?" Tiny asked again in a more forceful tone.

"I must have dropped it when he locked me in the grandfather clock at the new amusement park."

"What!"

This was not the reaction I was going for. "But I have a plan," I said, hoping Tiny would calm down, being more interested in my plan.

"What sort of plan?" he asked, letting out a slow exhale in contrast to his earlier outburst.

"You could text my phone about how you found something that could lead us to the murderer and how you want to meet me at the park."

"Set a trap for him," said Tiny.

"Exactly," I said.

"This could work."

"Mel, I don't think that it should just be us who do this," Greg added.

"Hey," interrupted Tiny, "my boys and I can handle this."

"I didn't mean—I think we should call Detective Shorts."

"We will," I said. "When Tiny sends that text, he'll send one to Detective Shorts too."

"It's all settled then," said Jackie.

Jon released a huge yawn, which I thought was weird for a ghost, but he might have just been trying to make a point, and said, "If we've all voted on what's to be done, can we get it over with? I'm a little tired of hanging out with you all."

"Are our personalities too small for you?" teased Jackie.

While Jackie and Jon got into another match of who could churn out the best insult, Tiny pulled out his phone and sent a text to mine and the detective. "Done," he said. "Let's roll."

Chapter 13

Jackie and I watched from behind a closed hot dog stand as Greg stood near the big grandfather clock, waiting in the dark for the mysterious man to show up, assuming he took the bait. Tiny, who hid elsewhere, had received no reply on his phone, so all we could do was hope that he had taken it.

Jackie sighed.

"Will you stop?" I whispered to her.

"I'm bored," she said. "We've been here for an hour and nothing has happened."

"It's only been forty-five minutes."

"Big difference."

Greg turned and looked at me, and judging by his stance, I knew that he thought the same as Jackie: the man was not coming.

"Another ten minutes and we're leaving," I said.

"Deal."

I didn't blame her for wanting to go. Even I began to think that the ruse had not worked. Why would he make us wait for almost an hour if he planned on meeting us? Or did he figure out that we planned on setting a trap for him? I glanced around, but saw no sign of Tiny or Detective Shorts. Though, if the detective had replied to Tiny's text, that didn't mean that Tiny would say anything. He did not like cops very much, and when you sometimes operate outside of the law, I can see why, but a part of me wondered if there was a more personal reason that he refused to delve into.

The heel of a boot scraped the sidewalk. I looked around, doing my best to remain hidden, as I tried to locate the source of the sound. Greg's sudden attentive stance told me that he had heard it too. I nudged Jackie and motioned for her to crouch even further behind the hot dog stand. We watched as a man approached Greg, walking with caution while trying to appear as though he was not apprehensive at all.

"Tiny?" said the man.

I pulled out Jackie's phone, which she had lent to me earlier, and pressed the record button.

"Who are you?" demanded Greg, doing a good job of pretending to be surprised that it wasn't me walking up to him.

"Mel, sent me."

Typical reply.

"She did?" Greg's skeptical response caused the man to move closer.

"Yeah, she couldn't make it and asked me to come. So what's this thing you've got?"

"I don't know what you're talking about."

"Yes, you do."

"Another time."

"Hey, man," said the man, getting a little pushy, "I'm doing you both a favor."

"Keep your favors," said Greg. "I'll wait until she isn't too busy to meet me herself."

"What's he doing?" Jackie whispered to me.

I motioned for her to stay silent. I didn't want the man to know we were there.

"Give me what I've come for." The man pulled out a gun and pointed it at Greg, stopping him and I had to use my free hand to support the one holding Jackie's phone so that it would quit shaking.

"Hey, man, I don't want any trouble," Greg replied.

"Neither do I. You texted this phone"—he pulled out my cell and waved it in front of Greg—"saying that you had something that could link you to me. I want it."

"Why'd you do it?"

The man stared at Greg. "Do what?"

"Kill that man in the clock."

"I didn't kill that stupid midget."

"If you had nothing to do with it," said Greg, backing away, "then why are you here?"

"It's for what I am planning to do," said the man.

"And what's that?" Greg continued to back away.

"Why would I tell you? You'll just turn me in."

"Not likely," replied Greg. "We both know that you're not going to let me walk out of here."

The man sneered. "How perceptive of you. All right, if you insist. There is a man who deserves death."

"You plan to carry that out." Greg took another step back. "Stop right there."

Greg's arm moved, but I could not make out what he held in his hand.

"I said stop!"

Greg lifted his arm up and the flash from his phone's camera went off, blinding the man just as he raised his gun. When the light dissipated, Greg had gone and the man stood alone, screaming in frustration.

"Where is he?" Jackie whispered to me.

"I don't know," I replied, checking the footage that I had just recorded, "but I think we should go."

We crawled out from behind the hot dog stand, but just as Jackie tried to stand up, her foot caught on the stand's cover and she fell over, taking the canvass cover with her. "MEEP!" she screamed and covered her mouth after the noise had escaped her lips.

The man turned in our direction. I didn't need daylight to tell me that he saw us, or what he planned to do next.

He bolted for us.

I knelt down and freed Jackie's foot from the hot dog stand's cover, grabbed her arm, and helped her up. We ran down the walk and towards the big quad where the majority of the rides were.

Where was Greg?

I didn't have time to worry about that and hoped he had managed to get away. I glanced behind me. The man quickened his pace and closed in on us fast.

"Hurry!" I yelled at Jackie.

She glanced behind her, her eyes widened, and ran faster. "Where do we go?"

The lights in the park turned on and music played over the loudspeakers. For a split second, I wondered who could have turned everything on, but I had no time to ponder it. I spotted the Ferris Wheel.

"Over here!" I shouted.

Jackie followed me. "What now?" she asked when we reached the Ferris Wheel.

"Get on." I lifted the bar to one of the seats and pushed her on.

"I don't think this is a good ide—"

"We can't outrun him!"

I ran to the controls and pulled the lever, turning on the Ferris Wheel. Its lights sparked to life, blinking in some singsong fashion as a different sort of music played form the speakers surrounding it. As it warmed up and the seats began to move, I ran to the carriage Jackie sat in and jumped in just as it rose into the air. As I sat up, I caught my breath and watched as the man stopped below us, fuming over losing us, and grew smaller as we went higher.

"You do realize that we will end up back on the bottom, right?" said Jackie.

Yeah. I didn't think this part all the way through.

"Can you send a quick message to Tiny, Greg, or Detective Shorts?" I asked.

Jackie nodded and pulled out her phone as we reached the top and started our descent.

The ride stopped.

"What was that?" asked Jackie.

I shrugged. There was no reason for it to cease working all the sudden and the man who had chased us seemed just as confused. He strode over to the controls and pulled the lever, starting the Ferris Wheel again, but the lever moved itself back into the off position and our seat jerked as the ride stopped again swinging us back and forth. The man pulled the lever again and once more, we went downward. I watched as the lever snapped back into the off position, and for a third time, we stopped, the sudden movement jostling out seat.

"You know, this isn't helping my stomach any," commented Jackie.

Jon! It had to be him.

Frustrated, the man kicked the console and approached the ride, reaching up and grabbing the rungs of a ladder built into the side of the structure.

"What's he doing?" asked Jackie as we watched.

"Climbing," I said.

"How?"

I pointed at the ladder that was most likely used by maintenance personnel and my heart fell as I watched him come closer.

"Now what?" Jackie asked, voicing the same question I had.

I glanced around, but found nothing we could use or do to get out of there. For a moment, I considered using the built-in ladder on the side of the Ferris Wheel, but changed my mind when I realized there was no way for us to get to it without risking a fall. He came closer. A little panicked, I looked at Jackie with a hopeless expression just when the ride turned back on and we descended to the ground in a hurry. Once we came to a stop, I lifted the bar and jumped off the seat, taking Jackie with me. A shot went off, striking the window of a food stand as we passed. Taking a quick glance back, I watched as the man scrambled down the ladder and continued chasing us, but saw no sign of Jon.

"Look!" Jackie said, pointing at the fun house.

"Oh, I hate those," I moaned. "Isn't there someplace else we can—"

Another gunshot stopped me from finishing my sentence. Jackie ran ahead of me into the fun house while I tripped over the steps leading into it. I stopped cold. I hadn't been in here before and had no idea where to go or how to navigate the maze of glass before me.

"This way," hissed Jackie as she walked between the panels of glass with confidence.

"Do you know where you are going?" I asked her.

"I came in here when we came here together to enjoy the park. That was before I ran into Tammy."

I followed Jackie through the narrow path, going around corners and between panels of glass, some of which, though not all, when looked through, made everything seem a bit distorted. Heavy footsteps pounded the stairs in the entrance and I knew that the man had arrived. He entered the fun house and the footsteps stopped. I didn't need to turn around to know that he analyzed the situation, trying to figure out the best way to get to us.

"Turn to your left," Jackie said to me.

I did, passing through another narrow walkway lined with glass that didn't seem to be there because it was so clear and clean, a stark contrast to some of the fogged panels I had passed earlier.

The footsteps started again, informing me that he had begun his trek through the fun house.

I looked back. The man stood there, with several walls of glass between us, glaring at us. He bolted. Oh no! I just remembered that he worked here and might have been in the fun house a few times himself and knew the way through.

"Jackie, we need to hurry."

"I forgot which way to go," said Jackie.

"Just pick one." I watched as the man neared, turning corners.

"Now I remember. Go right."

I went right.

"Left!"

I turned left.

For the next few seconds I made several turns, feeling as though I went in circles, as I followed Jackie's instructions.

"Left again," said Jackie.

I went left and ran into a panel of glass, generating a thud that echoed throughout the fun house.

"Sorry," Jackie apologized. "I meant right. Your other left."

I almost chuckled at that comment, but just as I looked up and rubbed my head from where I had bumped it, I shrieked. Right in front of me, with only a piece of glass between us, was the man we had been running from. He glowered at me and the stony expression on his face told me all I needed to know: he intended to kill us. He raised his weapon and pointed it at the glass.

"Jackie, run!" I screamed and hurried away, slamming into another glass panel as I felt my way around it and shoved Jackie onward.

The man fired.

The gunshot reverberated around the chamber, echoing for several minutes, hurting our ears. I covered mine and winced from the deafening noise, but my feet kept moving, scraping the back of Jackie's heels. Another gunshot rang out. I looked back. The man fired at the glass panels, shattering them and clearing a path for himself as glass flew in every direction.

The lights flickered.

The man destroyed another panel of glass, ignoring the dimming lights as he focused on getting to us.

They flickered again, this time, turning off for ten seconds before turning back on.

The man stopped. He glanced around, a perplexed expression on his face, wondering why the lights acted in such a strange manner, but I knew why: Jon had arrived.

The man raised his weapon, aiming for me as I stood there, watching the spectacle.

The lights turned off.

In a flurry of movement, Jackie grabbed my shoulder and wrenched me to the side, shoving me along as she fed me directions for which way to turn while the lights flashed back on and flickered at such a rapid rate that my head spun, followed by the man's frightened screams. Jon moved around him, surrounding him, and somehow made it appear as though there were more of him. He taunted the man as he fired his gun until it ran out of bullets, and in a last attempt to free himself of this terror, he threw his weapon, which smashed into a wall, shattering three glass panels and sending shards of glass various directions.

Jackie and I turned another corner and I spotted the exit. We quickened our pace and burst through the doors, with the man right behind us.

"Duck!" came Greg's voice.

I grabbed Jackie and forced her to the ground just as a steel bar swung over us and struck the man in the face. He crumpled to the ground.

"Hey, I wanted to do that," said Jon in a disappointed tone.

Though Greg couldn't see him, he must have heard him because he held out the steel bar, saying, "Be my guest."

The bar left Greg's hands and moved by itself through the air, striking the man with a solid *thunk*.

"OOO," said Jackie. "That's going to leave a mark."

"Where'd you go?" I asked Greg.

"I knew I had to get away from him, but once I did, I turned to find that you two had gone. So, I searched the park for you. The constant turning on and off of the lights in the fun house told me you might be here."

"My hero." I kissed Greg.

"Oh, yeah, he's the hero," griped Jon, who solidified and parked himself on our pursuer's back, "because I didn't do anything. Oh, well. I'll just sit here and guard this piece of excrement while you two go about your business. No need to thank me, either."

"Thank you," I said to Jon. "Oh, Tiny!"

I yanked out Jackie's phone, which I still had with me, and dialed Tiny's number, my heart falling as it continued to ring before going to voicemail. I hung up and dialed his number again and again and each time it went to voicemail, while multitudes of horrific scenarios played through my mind about what might have happened to him. "Tiny, please pick up."

"I'm here," mumbled Tiny, rubbing his head and leaning on Detective Short's shoulder.

I ran to him and gave him a hug. "What happened?"

"That idiot got the drop on me and knocked me out," answered Tiny.

"And tricked me into going into a maintenance shed where he locked me in," added Detective Shorts. "I didn't get out until Tiny woke up."

"This is all so heartwarming," quipped Jon, "but shouldn't we lock this guy up?"

Detective Shorts placed the man in custody and before he walked away, he reminded us that, "I'll need to get all of your statements, so none of you leave."

"That's not happening," said Jon as he disappeared in front of the detective, who got a shocked look on his face. He must have thought that Jon was real. "Testimonies from ghosts don't hold up well in court, or so I'm told. Not that you would want anyone to know that a ghost saved all of your behinds."

"I'll meet you all back at the station." Detective Shorts walked off, dragging the groggy would be murderer.

"Oh crap!" shouted Jackie and we all turned to her in surprise as she was not one to swear.

"What?" I asked her.

"That talent show is tomorrow!"

I stared at her in bewilderment.

"Mr. Stilton is expecting me to perform a ventriloquist act, remember?"

Now I remembered. "Let's discuss that on the way to the police station."

"You're a ventriloquist?" asked Tiny as we walked away. "Really?"

Chapter 14

I sat in the audience, staring at the stage, watching the show being performed while I waited for Jackie's routine. We had spent all night convincing Jon to help us out and he finally agreed after I reminded him that he was the reason we were in this predicament to begin with.

"Hey," said Greg as he sat down. "Sorry I'm late."

"So, what did you find out?"

"The man that showed up last night is Alfred Monark and is Tony Dribbens' cousin. Their mothers were sisters, but when they married, their last names changed, which is why we didn't put it together right away. According to Jack, they had been close as children, but when Dribbens was sent away for murder, Monark was out of the country, working on an oil rig. He didn't learn about any of it until he returned to the country. After that, he vowed to get revenge and then just disappeared."

"So he was after Detective Shorts," I said.

"No, that's just it," replied Greg, "he wasn't. There was a warden at the prison who mistreated Dribbens to such a degree that it drove him to commit suicide. That is whom Monark blamed for his cousin's death."

"Boy, were we on the wrong track," I said.

"Not necessarily."

"And Henry Farford?"

"Monark's first murder. He confessed to killing him. Farford was friends with Dribbens' cellmate and his friend told him everything. So, he agreed to help Monark get revenge, but got cold feet when it was time to go through with it. Monark killed him to keep him from talking, and since he was known as the town drunk, no on batted an eye when his place burned down."

"The things people do," I muttered. "How is it Jack learned all this?"

"He eavesdropped through the interrogation room's security camera."

I smiled. "You'd think they would learn not to let your cousin near a computer."

"Good thing they haven't."

"Will you two shut up?" growled someone behind us.

Greg and I closed our mouths and scrunched down in our seats, watching the show."

"Next up," said the announcer, "is Jackie and her little friend!"

The audience did a polite series of claps as Jackie stepped on stage, carrying Jon, who had managed to make himself visible for everyone as he pretended to be a dummy.

"You know, I don't like being called your 'little friend'," Jon said as Jackie sat in the chair provided for her.

"Well, you're not exactly tall."

"I have a name, you know."

"What's that? Grouchy?"

"Excuse me?"

"You're such a grouchy dwarf."

"Perhaps you need glasses."

"Why's that?"

"Because you squint all the time. No wonder you guys never see that giant lizard coming to terrorize your cities. You can't see, so you squint like this before yelling, 'Godzilla!'"

"Hey, Grumpy," Jackie shot back, "the producer from *Snow White and the Seven Dwarves* called, wanting to know when you will be back on the set."

"Yeah, well, Jackie Chan said he doesn't want you in any more of his movies. Your Kung Fu isn't good enough. Basically, he fired you."

"He can't fire me. I quit!"

"Yeah, well, I can't quit my job."

"Why's that?"

"They fired me."

"Why did they fire you?" asked Jackie.

"It's embarrassing," said Jon.

"Come on."

Jon looked around before leaning close to Jackie. "I was too tall."

"What?"

"They wanted someone who is three-six and I'm three-eight. That's just two freaking inches!"

I glanced around as the crowd laughed at Jackie's performance, something she seemed to be a natural at.

"It this skit socially acceptable?" asked Greg as she and Jon started trading insults again.

"Who cares?" I replied. "What are people going to do, sue a ghost? Something tells me that it won't work out so well as bad things tend to happen when you anger a ghost. Just think of what Rachel does to all the people who make her mad."

Greg nodded his head and turned back to the performance while we received another harsh "SHH!" from the person behind us.

I glanced at Mr. Stilton who had shown up, making sure that Jackie and I were not putting him on when we mentioned her being in the talent show. He had a huge smile on his face and seemed to be enjoying himself. Well, that was another crisis avoided. I turned back to Jackie's and Jon's act, looking forward to an uneventful day at work tomorrow.

Well… one can always hope.

Look for book 13 in the series

Coming Soon

About the Author

Janet McNulty currently lives in West Virginia where she continues to work on the Mellow Summers Series. She began the series two years ago as a fluke, but liked writing it so much, that she decided to stick with it.

Besides writing paranormal mysteries, Ms. McNulty has also accomplished success in other genres. She has a fantasy saga (*Legends Lost*) published under the name of Nova Rose and a new dystopian trilogy (*Dystopia*) and acience fiction series (*Solaris Saga*) as well. Ms. McNulty once referred to herself as an author who is "a little something for everyone."

She is currently busy working on the next Mellow Summers book.

Of course, writing is not the only passion in her life and every author needs some down time. When she isn't working on her books, Ms. McNulty enjoys reading and just poking around in her garden.

More by Janet McNulty

The Mellow Summers Series

Sugar And Spice And Not So Nice
Frogs, Snails, And A Lot Of Wails
An Apple A Day Keeps Murder Away
Three Little Ghosts
Oh Holy Ghost
Where Trouble Roams
Two Ghosts Haunt A Grove
Trick Or Treat Or Murder
Roses Are Red…He's Dead
Double, Double, Nothing But Trouble
Ring Around The Rosy, Not Another Ghosty
Hickory Dickory Dock The Ghost In The Clock

Mellow Summers moves to Vermont to attend college, accompanied by her friend Jackie. They soon find themselves running into ghosts and one mystery after another.

The Solaris Saga

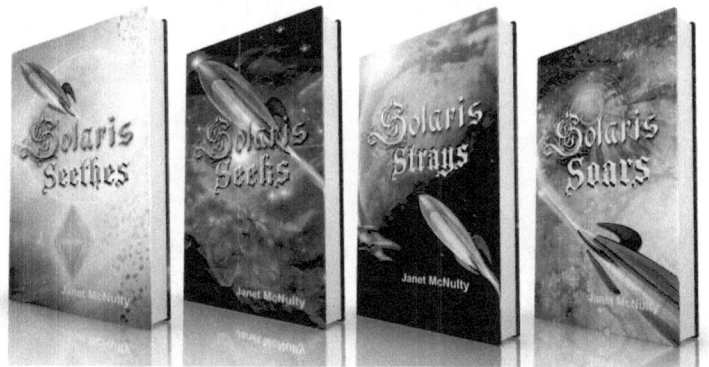

Solaris Seethes
Solaris Seeks
Solaris Strays
Solaris Soars

Every myth has a beginning.

After escaping the destruction of her home planet, Lanyr, with the help of the mysterious Solaris, Rynah must put her faith in an ancient legend. Never one to believe in stories and legends, she is forced to follow the ancient tales of her people: tales that also seem to predict her current situation.

Forced to unite with four unlikely heroes from an unknown planet (the philosopher, the warrior, the lover, the inventor) in order to save the Lanyran people, Rynah and Solaris embark on an adventure that will shatter everything Rynah once believed.

The Legends Lost Series

Published under Nova Rose

Tesnayr
Amborese
Galdin

Enter the Lands of Tesnayr and join on an epic fantasy adventure that spans over 1,500 years.

Begin with Tesnayr, the first king of the five lands as he unites the against a savage foe bent on their destruction.

Next, Join Amborese as she fights reclaim the throne after her family was forced to flee from it.

Thinking peace has finally entered the land, follow Galdin as he returns to Tesnayr to find it greatly hanged. Barbarians, led by a mysterious sorcerer, burn and destroy as they go. And only Galdin can stop them if he chooses to accept his fate.

Visit www.legendslosttrilogy.com to learn more about the Legends Lost Trilogy.

The Dystopia Trilogy

Dystopia (Book 1)
Tempered Steel (Book 2)
Liberty's Torch (Book 3)

**Imagine living in a world where
everything you do is controlled.**

Dana Ginary lives in a world where every aspect of her life is controlled by the Dystopian Government. Forced to work in Waste Management, her life becomes a nightmare with hunger and survival is her only constant. Before she knows it, she is caught up in a resistance movement and exiled from Dystopia, forced to find her way in the barren wastelands. While there, she must learn to live independently and discover how far she is willing to go to live and achieve freedom.

Something for the Little Ones

The Dragon Who series

The Dragon Who was Afraid of the Dark
The Dragon Who Went to the Moon
The Dragon Who Found a Monster Party
The Dragon Who Found a Spider in His Shoe
The Dragon Who Explored the Sea
The Dragon Who Caught a Cold

The Fairy Who series

The Fairy Who Lost a Tooth
The Fairy Who Got Lost

The Mr. Chili series

Mr. Chili's Chili
Mr. Chili Goes To School
Mr. Chili's Halloween
Mr. Chili's Christmas

Others:

Mrs. Duck and the Dragon
The Hungry Washing Machine
Rhymes-a-lot
Are You the Monster Under My Bed?
How Do You Catch An Alien

Grandpa's Stories

My grandfather grew up in Arizona during the 1920s and 1930s. One week after the attack on Pearl Harbor he joined the Navy. During the summer of 2012, my mother visited him and recorded his stories about growing up, World War II, and his time as an employee at the Pacific Bell Telephone Company. This is the history of the 20th century as he lived it. These recordings make up this book. These are his words.

www.ingramcontent.com/pod-product-compliance
Lightning Source LLC
Chambersburg PA
CBHW020639180626
46816CB00003B/1039